MIKE CAVALLARO

Color by Irene Yeom

First Second
NEW YORK

First Second

Published by First Second
First Second is an imprint of Roaring Brook Press,
a division of Holtzbrinck Publishing Holdings Limited Partnership
120 Broadway, New York, NY 10271
firstsecondbooks.com
mackids.com

Library of Congress Control Number: 2023933096

First edition, 2024
Edited by Mark Siegel and Dennis Pacheco
Cover design and interior book design by Sunny Lee and Yan L. Moy
Production editing by Arik Hardin
Color by Irene Yeom

This book was drawn using a Gryphon Claw Stylus and an Artikus Maximus tablet,
Platinum Edition, which was custom made by Vulcan himself in his workshop on the island of Celestina.
Irene colored the whole thing using various spells from Chromosius Goachely's well-known
Grimoire of Practical & Theoretical Pigmentalization.

Printed in China by Toppan Leefung Printing Ltd., Dongguan City, Guangdong Province

ISBN 978-1-250-84643-3 (paperback)
1 3 5 7 9 10 8 6 4 2

ISBN 978-1-250-84644-0 (hardcover)
1 3 5 7 9 10 8 6 4 2

1
EVERYTHING
is EVERYTHING.

ROUGHLY TWO DOZEN ARROWS.
BOTH MY THROWING AXES.
VARIOUS SPELLS AND A GARDEN'S WORTH OF SPECTRAL VINES.
IT BARELY SLOWED HIM DOWN.
IN THE END, IT TOOK BRINGING DOWN THE CEILING WITH A BLAST FROM MY MYSTIC SWORD JUST TO HOLD HIM IN PLACE.
THAT GAVE SULTANA ENOUGH TIME TO FIND THE RUNE KING'S PHYLACTERY AND DESTROY IT WITH A WHACK FROM THE STAR HAMMER.
LOOKS LIKE THAT'S THE END OF THE STAR HAMMER, BUT IT'S ALSO THE END OF THE RUNE KING.
IT WAS A GOOD PLAN, AND IT WORKED. BUT LEMME TELL YA, IF YOU EVER HAVE TO GO UP AGAINST AN UNDEAD LICH OF IMMENSE POWER, AVOID BEING PART OF THE DIVERSION. IT HURTS.

ONCE LANSELOS HAD CAUGHT HIS BREATH, WE TORCHED THE RUNE KING'S LAIR AND HEADED BACK TO TURGONVILLE.
WE KNEW THE TOWNSFOLK WOULD BE PSYCHED TO HEAR THEIR TROUBLES WITH THE LICH WERE FINALLY OVER.

WE WERE LOOKING FORWARD TO A LITTLE REST AND RELAXATION, AND I COULDN'T WAIT TO SPEND SOME OF THE REWARD MONEY WE HAD COMING TO US.
I WOULD HAVE OFFED THAT LICH FOR FREE, BUT LET'S FACE IT, ADVENTURING AIN'T CHEAP. I HAD TWO GOOD THROWING AXES TO REPLACE, FOR STARTERS.

BUT OUR VACATION WOULD HAVE TO WAIT.
OUR NEXT JOB HAD ALREADY SHOWN ITS FACE.
FEAST OR FAMINE, AS THE SAYING GOES.

AT THE END OF THE DAY, IT'S STILL A GOOD WAY TO MAKE A LIVING.
ATTENTION:
Knights, Paladins, Fighters, Healers, Rangers &
ADVENTURERS
of all Breeds:
The Goode People of Sheep's Eddy offer Rich Reward for the Rescue & Return of our Prince from the clutches of the Diabolical Sorceror who plagues our goode land.
Payment in Coin, Etc. upon completion.
Serious Inquiries Only.
Follow Willow River north. Sheep's Eddy is on the east bank across from the three flat hills. You can't miss it.
Signed, The Goode People of Sheep's Eddy
MAYBE SOMEDAY I'LL GET TO DO THIS *FOR REAL.*
RIGHT NOW, THIS *GAME* IS AS CLOSE AS I CAN GET.
...AAAAND WE'RE GOING TO *STOP* THERE UNTIL NEXT TIME!

LET ME INTRODUCE MY *FRIENDS...*
THAT *ROCKED,* PHOEBE.
THANKS.
THIS IS *PHOEBE...*
VEDA...
LANCE...
WHAT A *BLOODBATH.* ONE MORE HIT AND I'D BE *DEAD.*
IF I'D LOST THAT *SAVING THROW,* WE'D *ALL* BE DEAD.
AND *STEPHIE.*

OUR FAMILIES HAVE KNOWN EACH OTHER *FOREVER.* THEY'RE THE SIBLINGS I NEVER HAD, AND WE DO PRETTY MUCH *EVERYTHING* TOGETHER.
WHEN WE FIRST STARTED *GAMING,* IT WAS AT SOMEONE ELSE'S HOUSE EVERY WEEK.
BUT EVENTUALLY, WE SETTLED ON *MINE* BECAUSE...
WELL, BECAUSE *LOOK AT IT.*

HEY, WAS THIS HERE LAST TIME?

UNLESS IT MOVED ON ITS OWN...

OH WAIT, THAT'S RIGHT. NOW I REMEMBER.
IT'S FROM GALAXY HUNTER 4, RIGHT?
YUP.

I GUESS I JUST CAN NEVER REMEMBER WHICH SCENE IT'S IN.
C'MON, STEPHIE, I'VE TOLD YOU A MILLION TIMES- IT GOT CUT!
NONE OF THIS STUFF EVER GOT USED. THAT'S HOW MY DAD GOT IT TO BEGIN WITH.
NONE OF THIS IS TRUE, BUT THE TRUTH IS HARD TO EXPLAIN, AND THEY'D STILL NEVER BELIEVE IT.
NOT EVEN THESE, MY CLOSEST FRIENDS. MY EXTENDED FAMILY.

WHAT'S YOUR DAD WORKING ON *NOW?*
OH, YOU KNOW HOW ***HOLLYWOOD*** IS. EVERYTHING'S A ***BIG SECRET,*** BLAH, BLAH, BLAH.
HE'S LIKE... NOT ALLOWED TO TALK ABOUT IT.
ANOTHER LIE. I DON'T LIKE IT, BUT IT'S FOR THE BEST.

MY ***RIDE'S*** HERE. ANYONE NEED A LIFT?

WE ALL RODE BIKES.
SO? THROW THEM IN THE TRUNK.

THE ***DRIVERLESS CAR*** THING STILL FREAKS ME OUT A LITTLE.
SUIT YOUR-SELVES.
SEE YA TOMORROW, PHEEBS.

SEE YA!
LATER, E!

DID YOU GET THAT LICH?
THE LICH IS TOAST.

WE WENT AFTER ITS PHYLACTERY.
IS THAT HOW IT WOULD HAVE WORKED IN REAL LIFE?

IN REAL LIFE? I ONLY HAD TO TACKLE A LICH ONCE, AND THINGS GOT HAIRY FAST-
STOP PUTTING IDEAS IN HER HEAD AND COME INSIDE.

DINNER'S ON THE TABLE.
I WAS JUST SAYING-

BETWEEN YOU AND THAT GAME OF THEIRS, THAT'S ENOUGH TALK OF MAYHEM AND SLAUGHTER FOR ONE DAY.
IT'S DINNER TIME, AND THEN EOWULF NEEDS TO START GETTING READY FOR BED.
YOU KNOW WHAT TOMORROW IS.
DON'T REMIND ME.

AS I WAS SAYING, YOU COULD TAKE A LICH, THE QUESTION IS—WOULD IT STAY DEAD?

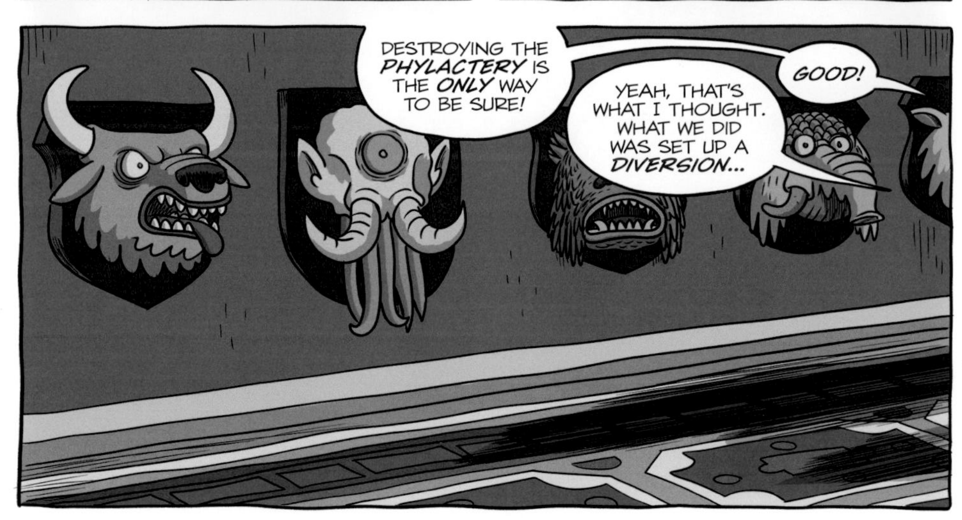
DESTROYING THE PHYLACTERY IS THE ONLY WAY TO BE SURE!
GOOD!
YEAH, THAT'S WHAT I THOUGHT. WHAT WE DID WAS SET UP A DIVERSION...

BRRRT!
BRRRT!
BRRRT!
BRRRT!
BRRRT!
BRR--
CLIK!
5:00 AM

KLIK!

SO...

...LIKE I WAS SAYING...

...THE TRUTH IS HARD TO EXPLAIN.
AND WHO WOULD BELIEVE IT?

YOU'RE LATE.

I'M READY.

OH?
Danger Level
4
5
6
7
8
9
10

WE'LL SEE...
KRANK!
3
4
5
6
7
8
9
10

HERE, LET'S BACK UP A LITTLE.
ZAM!
ZAM!
ZAM!
ZAM!

SLASH!
DING!
⟨10⟩
MY NAME IS ***EOWULF WEGMUND.***
ZA!
BREAK!
YEAH, YEAH. I KNOW. IT'S A ***FAMILY NAME.***

EOWULF, DAUGHTER OF DEOWULF...

...SON OF CEOWULF...

...DESCENDANT OF BEOWULF.
THAT'S RIGHT.
LEGENDARY MONSTER SLAYER.
ZA! ⟨10⟩
⟨10⟩
ZA!
ZA! ⟨10⟩
THAT BEOWULF.

PROTECT YOUR FLANK! DON'T OVEREXTEND!

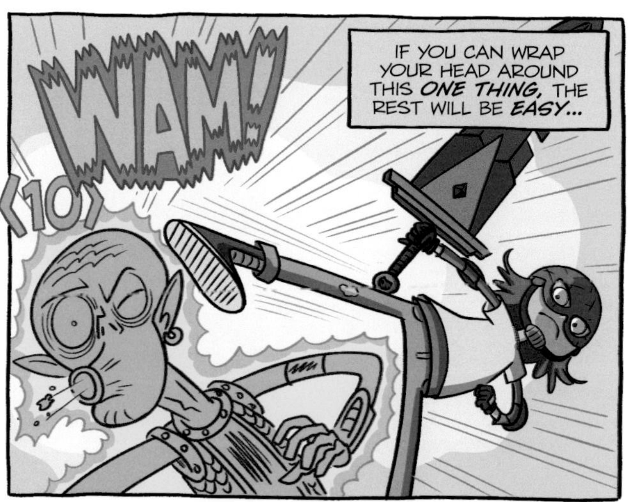
WAM!
IF YOU CAN WRAP YOUR HEAD AROUND THIS ONE THING, THE REST WILL BE EASY...
(10)

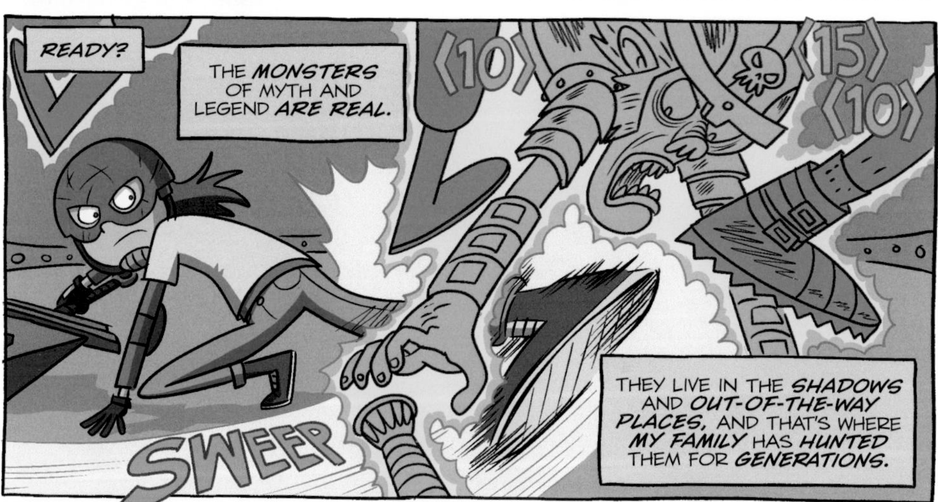
READY?
THE MONSTERS OF MYTH AND LEGEND ARE REAL.
(10)
(15)
(10)
THEY LIVE IN THE SHADOWS AND OUT-OF-THE-WAY PLACES, AND THAT'S WHERE MY FAMILY HAS HUNTED THEM FOR GENERATIONS.
SWEEP

THOSE TROPHIES ON THE WALLS UPSTAIRS AND ALL THE OTHER WEIRD STUFF AROUND THE HOUSE?
THOSE AREN'T UNUSED MOVIE PROPS LIKE I TELL MY FRIENDS. THEY'RE THE REAL DEAL.
YOU READY FOR THIS, ROGER?
I WAS BORN READY.

ZA!
(30)
ZRAKKA!
YOU AND ME BOTH, PARTNER!

SO, A WHILE BACK, I SET OUT TO JOIN THE FAMILY BUSINESS. YOU KNOW, BECOME THE GREATEST MONSTER HUNTER OF ALL.
LONG STORY, BUT NONE OF THAT WENT ACCORDING TO PLAN.

BUT I DISCOVERED SOMETHING.
SOMETHING IMPORTANT.

NOT ALL MONSTERS ARE **BAD.**
MY FAMILY HAD IT **ALL WRONG.**
TURNS OUT, IF YOU SPEND YOUR LIFE HUNTING **MYTHICAL CREATURES** BECAUSE THEY'RE **DIFFERENT** FROM YOU...
...GUESS WHAT?

HEADS UP, E! INCOMING!

KLASH!

YOU'RE THE MONSTER!
WHOA! WEIRD!
I TOLD YOU TO WATCH YOUR FLANK...

REVERSE SURGE, ROG!
COMING RIGHT UP!

KRR-ZAK!

SO I TURNED MY BACK ON ALL THAT. NO FOLLOWING IN ANYONE'S FOOTSTEPS FOR ME.
BONUS 40 SHAPE-SHIFTER

INSTEAD OF THAT...

...JUST A QUICK DIMENSIONAL SHIFT...
FWA!

SLAM!

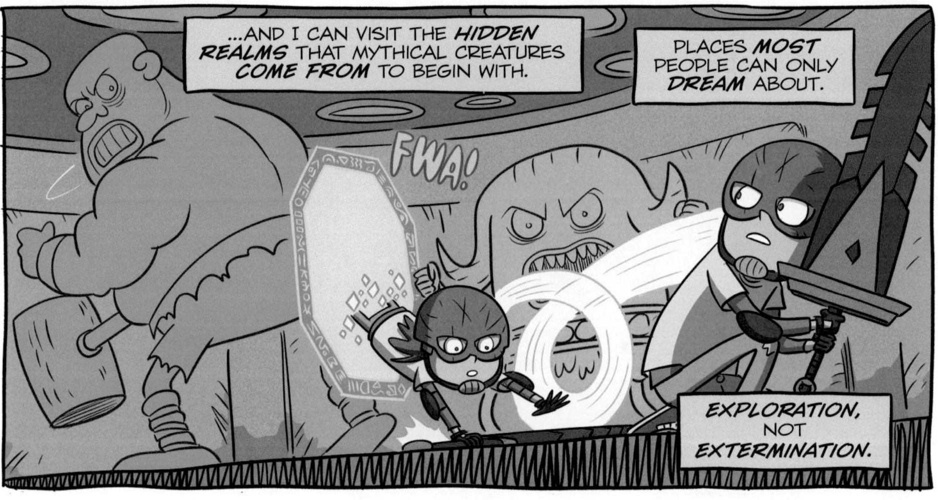
...AND I CAN VISIT THE HIDDEN REALMS THAT MYTHICAL CREATURES COME FROM TO BEGIN WITH.
PLACES MOST PEOPLE CAN ONLY DREAM ABOUT.
FWA!
EXPLORATION, NOT EXTERMINATION.

I KNOW WHAT YOU'RE THINKING. WHY ALL THE COMBAT TRAINING, THEN?

FIRST, BECAUSE THERE ARE STILL BAD THINGS OUT THERE.

AND SECOND, BECAUSE I'M GOOD AT IT.
ZA!
(50)

SO, IMAGINE YOU JUST HAD THE MOST AMAZING SUMMER VACATION EVER, ONLY INSTEAD OF THE BEACH OR WHATEVER...
...YOU SAVED A BUNCH OF UNICORN SOLDIERS FROM THE POCKET DIMENSION THEY WERE TRAPPED IN...
...MET THE KING AND QUEEN OF ATLANTIS...
...AND FOUGHT AN EVIL GOD TO SAVE THE MAGICAL SUPPLY SHOP AT THE CROSSROADS OF ALL REALITIES.
PRETTY RAD, HUH?
VULCAN'S CELESTIAL

BUT ALSO CRAZY-SOUNDING, RIGHT?
NOW YOU KNOW WHY I HAVE TO LIE TO MY FRIENDS.

NOW GO AHEAD AND ASK ME WHY I'D LEAVE REAL ADVENTURES LIKE THAT BEHIND TO PLAY IMAGINARY ONES WITH MY FRIENDS, AT HOME, IN NEW JERSEY.
SWA!

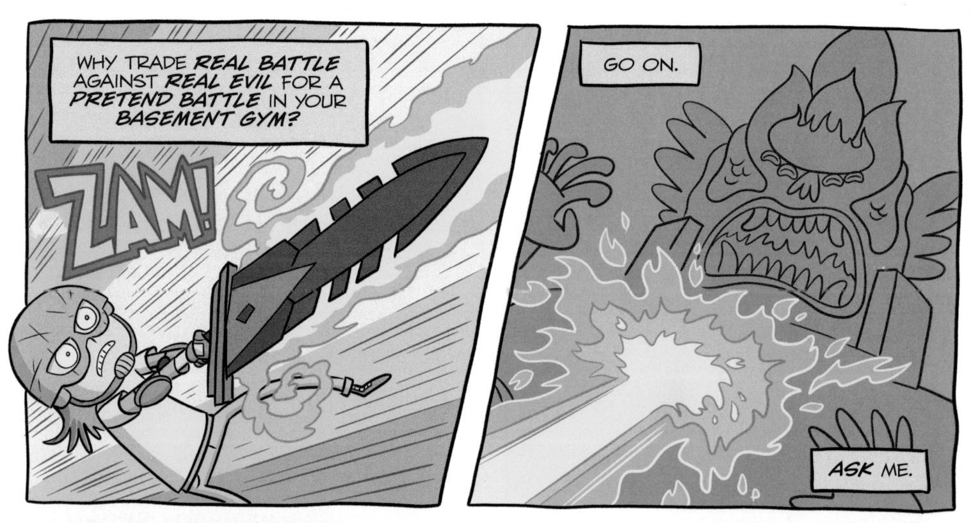
WHY TRADE REAL BATTLE AGAINST REAL EVIL FOR A PRETEND BATTLE IN YOUR BASEMENT GYM?
ZAM!
GO ON.
ASK ME.

WHAT IS GOING ON IN HERE?

DO YOU REALIZE WHAT TIME IT IS?
YOU'RE GOING TO BE LATE FOR SCHOOL!
AGAIN!
THAT'S WHY.
AW, MOM!
ZA!
ZA!
ZA!

MARCH!
SORRY, KIDDO...

DON'T APOLOGIZE TO HER, YOU'RE IN MORE TROUBLE THAN SHE IS! YOU'RE SUPPOSED TO BE THE ADULT HERE, REMEMBER?
AW...

MOM SHOWED UP JUST IN TIME. AHRIMAN WAS ABOUT TO CREAM YOU.

NO WAY! I HAD HIM ON THE ROPES!

HM. I DON'T KNOW ABOUT THAT.
I DO!

FFSSSSHHHH!

KRUNCH! KRUNCH!

ALL RIGHT, I'M OUT! SEE YA, MOM! SEE YA, DAD!
STOP RIGHT THERE!

WHAT IS THAT THING ON YOUR BACK?
MY BACKPACK?
RIGHT.

GO BACK UPSTAIRS AND GET RID OF THAT SWORD!
AW, MOM!
AND STOP SAYING THAT!

HOW MANY TIMES HAVE I TOLD YOU, IT'S A SCHOOL, NOT A BATTLEFIELD!

WHAT'S THE DIFFERENCE?
HURRY UP!

SORRY ABOUT THIS, *ROGER.*
ROGER'S A MAGIC SWORD I PICKED UP ON MY FIRST MISSION.

I KNOW I'VE ASKED THIS BEFORE, BUT ARE WE *CERTAIN* THESE ARE YOUR *REAL PARENTS?*

PRETTY SURE, YEAH.
BECAUSE DON'T FORGET THAT ONE TIME WITH THE *SHAPE-SHIFTER...*
EOWULF!

OKAY!
BUT HE'S NOT JUST A *WEAPON.* HE'S MY *FRIEND.* PROBABLY MY *BEST* FRIEND.

YEAH, THIS ISN'T *THAT,* PARTNER.
THE *ONLY ONE* WHO KNOWS THE *REAL ME.*

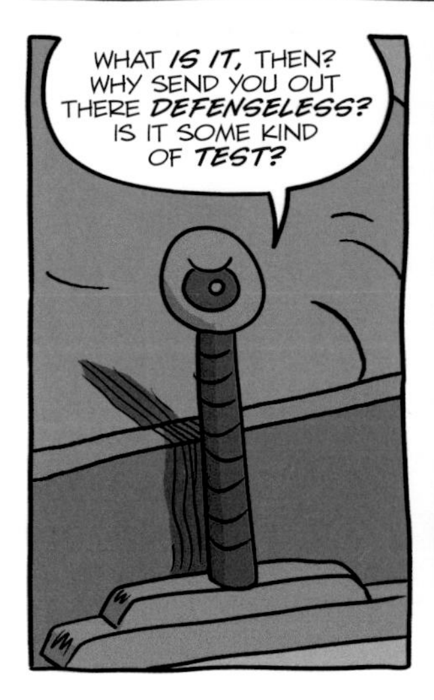
WHAT *IS IT,* THEN? WHY SEND YOU OUT THERE *DEFENSELESS?* IS IT SOME KIND OF *TEST?*

IT SURE *FEELS* THAT WAY.

I COULD USE SOME HELP, YOU KNOW.
WHAT'S THE PROBLEM?
GOODBYE!
BYE!

DON'T YOU THINK SHE'S BEEN A HANDFUL SINCE SHE GOT BACK?
OF COURSE, SHE'S A WULF.

SHE'S A CHILD.

SHE'S A WARRIOR.

WE'RE NOT AT WAR, DEE! WE'RE JUST TRYING TO RAISE A CHILD! IN NEW JERSEY!
YEAH, OUR WAY.

THE WAY I WAS RAISED. THE WAY WULFS HAVE BEEN RAISED FOR CENTURIES.

IT'S NOT HOW I WAS RAISED. DO I GET A SAY? EOWULF DOESN'T FEEL SHE BELONGS HERE. SHE NEEDS TO FIT IN.

SHE'S GOT HER FRIENDS. THEY MAKE A GOOD TEAM, THOSE KIDS.

SHE DOESN'T NEED A TEAM, SHE NEEDS NORMAL FRIENDS WHO DO NORMAL THINGS.
WHY?

UGH! YOU'RE JUST LIKE HER. THAT'S THE PROBLEM!

LOOK, I JUST NEED TO KNOW WE'RE ON THE SAME TEAM, OKAY?

I KNOW YOU'RE AN ANTIQUATED, HARDHEADED FISH OUT OF WATER, AND I LOVE YOU FOR IT. BUT WE WANT WHAT'S BEST FOR EOWULF, RIGHT?
OF COURSE.
GOOD. THEN STOP TRYING TO TAKE HER SIDE EVERY TIME I SAY SOMETHING. SHE'S FOUGHT UNICORNS AND BEEN WHO KNOWS WHERE, BUT NOW SHE HAS TO GO BACK TO SCHOOL LIKE A NORMAL PERSON, OKAY?

OKAY, OKAY!
SHE DIDN'T ACTUALLY FIGHT UNICORNS, THOUGH.
THEY WERE ON OUR SIDE.

I LOVE YOU, TOO!

GIVE IT BACK.
GO ON AND TAKE IT.
WELL? YA JUST GONNA STAND THERE?
CHICKEN.
YEAH, HE'S CHICKEN.

GIVE IT BACK, I SAID!
OOO! THE BIG BABY'S GETTING MAD, HUH?

ALL YOU GOTTA DO IS REACH UP AND TAKE IT, TWERP.

WHAT'S ALL THIS ABOUT?
OH, HEY, E. I WAS SURE YOU WERE GOING TO MISS THE BUS AGAIN.

DON'T TELL ME YOU SPENT ONE SUMMER OUT OF TOWN AND YOU ALREADY FORGOT THIS TIME-HONORED TRADITION.
I OUGHTA KNOCK YOU OUT.
YEAH, SOME THINGS ARE ETERNAL: SUNRISES, ACNE, HOMEWORK, AND PICKING ON AMADEUS HORNBURG.

LOOK AT HIM TAKE IT.
HE'S SO USED TO THIS, HE ALMOST LOOKS BORED.

WHAT'S GOING ON DOWN THERE? YOU KIDS BETTER NOT BE FIGHTING!

IT'S THIS FREAK'S FAULT, MRS. WALSKI!
SHOVE!

IT FIGURES! I SEE YOU, AMADEUS HORNBURG! DON'T YOU EVER GET TIRED OF MAKING TROUBLE?

I DIDN'T DO ANYTHING—
YOU'RE ALWAYS UP TO NO GOOD. YOUR POOR MOTHER WOULD BE ASHAMED!

WHY DON'T YOU MIND YOUR OWN BUSINESS, YOU OLD BAT?

YOU'RE A HORRIBLE CHILD! I'M GOING TO CALL THE SCHOOL!

SLAM!

GO AHEAD!

SEE?
SOMETIMES I'M TEMPTED TO FEEL BAD FOR HIM BECAUSE OF ALL THE GRIEF HE GETS, BUT SERIOUSLY?

THE KID'S A MONSTER.

VVVRRRRRRRRRRRRRRR!

KLAK!
STOP

SHLAK!

HERE'S YOUR *PRETTY JEWELRY,* WEIRDO.

HA HA!
OOOF!
HEY! WATCH IT!

WAP!
JERK! YOU DID THAT ON PURPOSE!
IDIOT!
SHOVE!

WHAT?

HORNBURG'S NOT THE *ONLY* MONSTER ON THIS BUS.

REALLY? YOU DIDN'T THINK SO LAST YEAR WHEN YOU GAVE HIM THAT BLACK EYE!
I DID?

WHAT? DID YOU FORGET?
NO!
I JUST.
I REMEMBER, BUT IT'S LIKE WATCHING SOMEONE ELSE DO IT.

OH, IT WAS YOU ALL RIGHT! MAN, YOU REALLY STOMPED HIM!

I KNOW, I KNOW.
BUT THAT WAS A DIFFERENT ME.

YEAH? HOW 'BOUT THE TIME BEFORE THAT?
AFTER THE PLANETARIUM TRIP?

HE STOLE THAT LITTLE ROCK I BOUGHT IN THE GIFT SHOP!

YEAH, BUT YOU PUNCHED HIM AFTER HE GAVE IT BACK!
BECAUSE THAT PROVED HE STOLE IT TO BEGIN WITH!

HEY, I THINK HE DESERVED IT. YOU'RE THE ONE BEING ALL WEIRD ABOUT IT.

WELL, WHY STEAL IT AT ALL, THEN?

BECAUSE, E, THAT'S WHAT MONSTERS DO.
A YEAR AGO, MAYBE, THAT ANSWER WOULD HAVE SATISFIED ME. BUT NOT ANYMORE.

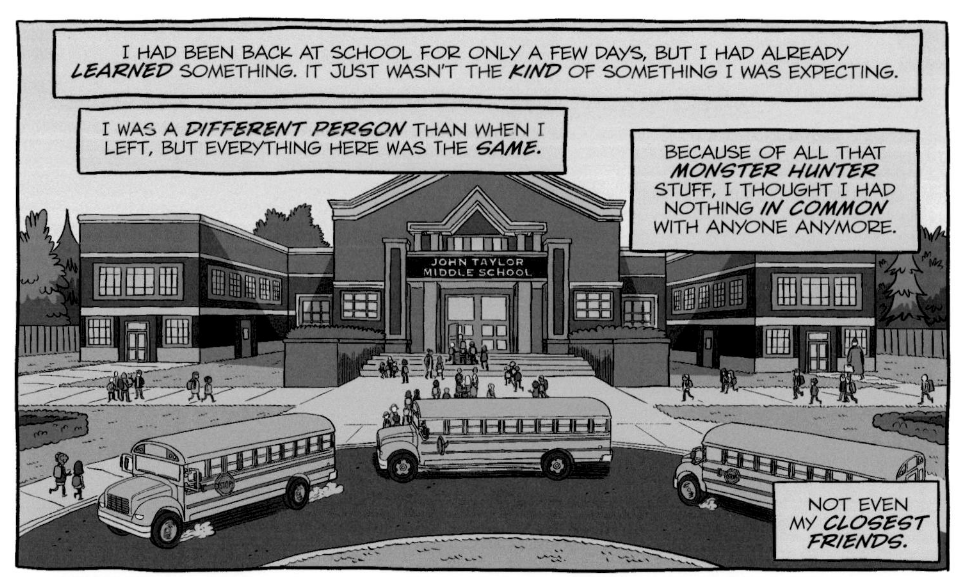
I HAD BEEN BACK AT SCHOOL FOR ONLY A FEW DAYS, BUT I HAD ALREADY *LEARNED* SOMETHING. IT JUST WASN'T THE *KIND* OF SOMETHING I WAS EXPECTING.
I WAS A *DIFFERENT PERSON* THAN WHEN I LEFT, BUT EVERYTHING HERE WAS THE *SAME.*
BECAUSE OF ALL THAT *MONSTER HUNTER* STUFF, I THOUGHT I HAD NOTHING *IN COMMON* WITH ANYONE ANYMORE.
JOHN TAYLOR MIDDLE SCHOOL
NOT EVEN MY *CLOSEST FRIENDS.*

BUT WATCHING *AMADEUS HORNBURG,* I REALIZED I HAD IT ALL *BACKWARDS.*
SPAK!
WE ALL HAD *TOO MUCH* IN COMMON.

SEE, WE'RE *ALL* MONSTER HUNTERS TO SOME DEGREE. IT'S IN OUR *DNA.*
WE *NEED* THEM.
AND IF THERE AREN'T ANY AROUND, WE *MAKE THEM UP.*
THUMP! THUMP! THUMP!
IN MY SCHOOL, IN MY TOWN, FOR *WHATEVER REASON,* AMADEUS WAS *"IT."*

AND IF ALL THAT WAS TRUE, THEN MAYBE I WASN'T AS OUT OF MY ELEMENT HERE AS I THOUGHT I WAS.
MAYBE I WAS JUST LOOKING AT IT WRONG.
TAKE THE LUNCH-ROOM, FOR EXAMPLE.

JUST A ROOMFUL OF KIDS, RIGHT?
FLIP!
BUT IF YOU HAD JUST ARRIVED FROM, SAY, ANOTHER DIMENSION, YOU MIGHT SEE A GATHERING OF SEPARATE AND DISTINCT GROUPS, EACH WITH THEIR OWN UNIFORMS, RULES, AND RITUALS.

THERE ARE MONSTERS HERE, TOO, AND MAYBE A FEW HEROES.
BUT IT'S HARD TO KNOW WHICH IS WHICH, AND SOME PEOPLE CAN BE BOTH, OR NEITHER.

THAT'S HOW MY ADVENTURES HAD LEFT ME FEELING, LIKE AN ALIEN VISITOR. OR LIKE ME, IN AN ALIEN PLACE.
SO MAYBE THAT WAS THE WAY TO APPROACH IT.

THIS DIDN'T *HAVE* TO BE THE BORING PAUSE BETWEEN ADVENTURES I ASSUMED IT WAS.
GO TA
WIL

IF I SIMPLY *DARED,* IT COULD BE THE START OF MY *GREATEST ONE.*

AND JUST LIKE *THAT...*
...I THOUGHT THAT MAYBE...
...MAYBE...
...I KNEW WHY I WAS THERE.

SPAK!

WHAT ARE YOU DRAWING?

SIGH...
WHAT DO YOU WANT?
NOTHING, I JUST-

HEY! THAT'S DR. HUMBARA FROM GILGAMESH 5000! THAT'S MY FAVORITE COMIC BOOK!
YOU'RE A PRETTY GOOD ARTIST!

I DIDN'T ASK WHAT YOU THOUGHT. AND ANYWAY, GILGAMESH 5000 IS BORING AND PREDICTABLE. THE DR. HUMBARA SPIN-OFF COMIC IS BETTER.

HM. I'VE NEVER READ THAT ONE. I MEAN...HE'S THE *BAD GUY*...

ONLY IN THE GILGAMESH COMIC. IN HIS *OWN* COMIC, HE CAN'T BE *DEFINED* BY SIMPLISTIC IDEAS OF *GOOD* OR *EVIL*.

WELL, THAT DEPENDS ON *WHAT HE DOES,* THOUGH, DOESN'T IT?
NO, IT DEPENDS ON *WHY HE DOES IT.*

WANT SOME *FRIES?*

I DON'T WANT *ANYTHING* FROM YOU. WHY ARE YOU *HERE?*

THAT'S KIND OF WHAT I'M TRYING TO FIGURE OUT...

WHAT'S UP, E?

IS "I'M-A-DOOFUS" HORNBURG BOTHERING YOU?

I BOTHER EVERYONE.

NO, HE'S NOT DOING ANYTHING-

THEN WHY ARE YOU HERE?

I ASKED HER THE SAME QUESTION.
SHUT UP, HORNHEAD. NO ONE'S TALKING TO YOU.

ACTUALLY, I'M TALKING TO HIM.

WHAT DID HE DO THIS TIME?
YEAH, E, WHAT DID HE DO THIS TIME?

GREAT GULA'S GHOSTS! WOULD YOU GUYS JUST GO EAT YOUR LUNCH AND LEAVE US ALONE FOR A MINUTE?
SNAP!

OKAY...?
WE'LL BE RIGHT OVER THERE...
IF YOU NEED US...

"GREAT GUGA'S" *WHAT?*
DON'T ASK *ME...*

YOU SHOULD TAKE YOUR OWN ADVICE.

WHAT DO YOU *MEAN?*
I'M TRYING TO *HELP* YOU.

YOU'RE HELPING ME?
YOU'RE HELPING ME?

WHAT-?
DUMP!
GRAB!

POK!

WHAT!
IS!
HAPPENING?!
I'LL CATCH HIM!

LEAVE HIM ALONE!
WAM!

WHAT IS *WRONG* WITH YOU TODAY?

I'M...

...GOING TO SEE IF I'VE GOT A CLEAN SHIRT IN MY GYM LOCKER...

IT COULD HAVE GONE *BETTER*...
DUMP!
...BUT YOU'VE GOT TO START *SOMEWHERE.*

⟨10⟩
ZA!
I DON'T SEE HOW IT COULD HAVE GONE ***WORSE,*** AND IT'S NOT CLEAR ***WHAT,*** EXACTLY, YOU'VE ***STARTED...***

THANKS. IS ***THAT*** ALL YOU HAVE TO SAY?
HARPIES, TWO O'CLOCK!

⟨20⟩
ZAM!
⟨20⟩
ZAM!

GET YOUR ***HEAD*** IN THE GAME, ***E.*** YOU'RE ***BARELY*** PAYING ***ATTENTION!***

HOW CAN I COMMENT ON YOUR ***STRATEGY*** WHEN I DON'T UNDERSTAND YOUR ***GOAL?***
IT'S ***NOT*** ALL ***GOALS*** AND ***STRATEGY,*** ROG!

I AM A SWORD!
SWAK!
(20)

I GET THAT, BUT I THOUGHT I EXPLAINED IT PRETTY WELL. WE'RE BACK IN ADVENTURE MODE, PARTNER!
HERE?!

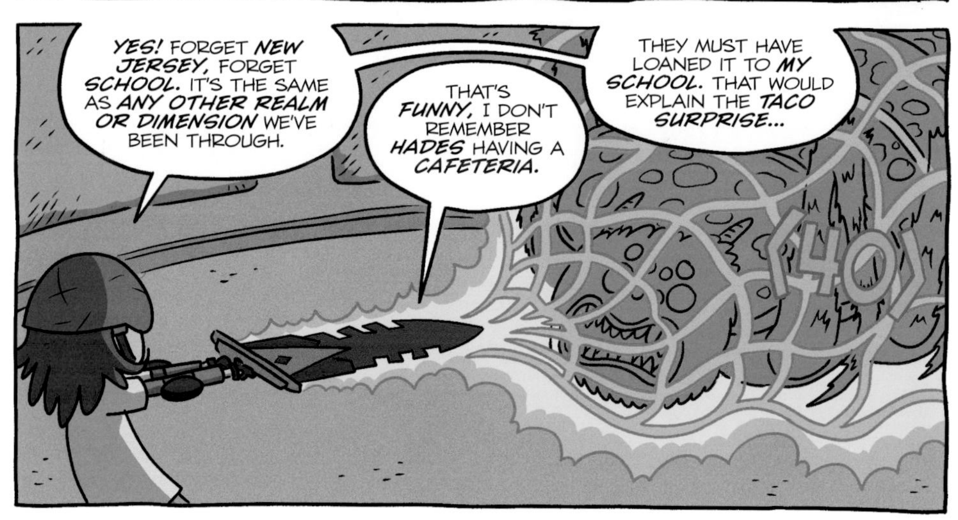
YES! FORGET NEW JERSEY, FORGET SCHOOL. IT'S THE SAME AS ANY OTHER REALM OR DIMENSION WE'VE BEEN THROUGH.
THAT'S FUNNY, I DON'T REMEMBER HADES HAVING A CAFETERIA.
THEY MUST HAVE LOANED IT TO MY SCHOOL. THAT WOULD EXPLAIN THE TACO SURPRISE...
(40)

COME ON, GUYS! LESS TALK, MORE ROCK!

BUT AMADEUS ISN'T A MYTHICAL CREATURE THAT NEEDS SAVING LIKE CERBERUS OR THOSE UNICORNS WERE.
SAYS WHO? WHAT'S THE DIFFERENCE?
STOMP!
STOMP!

FOR STARTERS, IT DOESN'T SOUND LIKE HE EVEN WANTS YOUR HELP.

STOMP!

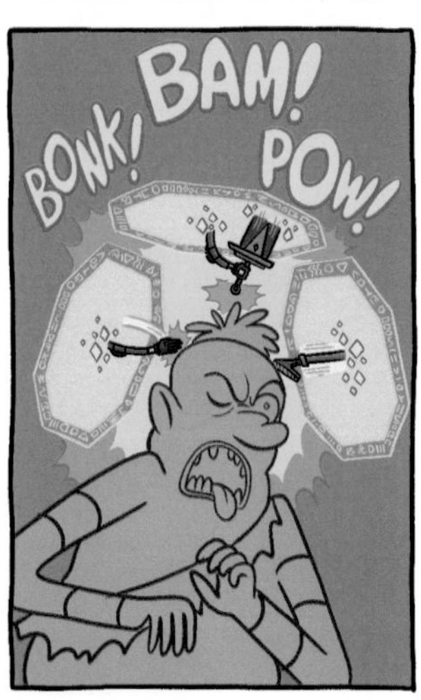
BONK!
BAM!
POW!

SO? NEITHER DID THE UNICORNS, AT FIRST.
(30)
THUD!

EOWULF, YOU SEE AMADEUS AS A VICTIM, BUT I THINK HE UNDERSTANDS HIS SITUATION BETTER THAN YOU DO, AND HE HAS A STRATEGY TO DEAL WITH IT.

I'LL REMIND YOU THAT YOU'RE THE ONE WHO LEFT COVERED IN ICED TEA.

WHAT STRATEGY? YOU MEAN GETTING BEATEN UP EVERY DAY?
⟨50⟩
ZA!
MASH!

I'M SAYING I THINK THERE'S MORE TO HIM THAN MEETS THE EYE. SOMETHING YOU SAID REALLY TRIGGERED HIM. WHY?
ALL I SAID WAS THAT I WAS TRYING TO HELP HIM, AND HE WENT BERSERK.

OKAY, THINK ABOUT THAT.
WHAT DO YOU MEAN? WHAT OTHER CHOICE DO I HAVE? JUST GO ON LETTING HIM GET BULLIED BY LITERALLY EVERYONE IN TOWN, EVERY DAY, FOREVER?
⟨10⟩
⟨10⟩
⟨10⟩

YOU'VE FOUGHT HIM MORE TIMES THAN WE CAN COUNT! YOU ARE THAT BULLY YOU'RE TALKING ABOUT, OR YOU'RE ONE OF THEM, AT LEAST!
⟨10⟩
⟨10⟩
⟨10⟩

RIGHT, THAT'S EXACTLY WHAT I'M TRYING TO FIX! I NEED TO DO THIS, ROG!
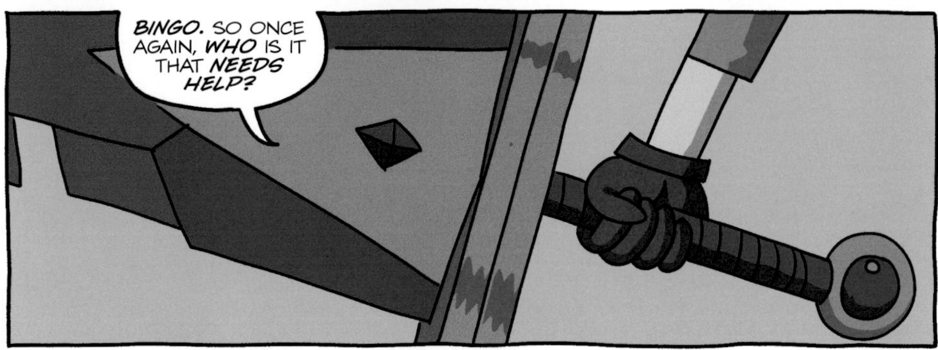
BINGO. SO ONCE AGAIN, WHO IS IT THAT NEEDS HELP?

WHAT? I–

OH...
OH!

OOOHHHHH....

WOW.

YEAH, I'M PRETTY SHARP, HUH?

UGH! THAT'S AN AWFUL PUN. WAY TO RUIN A MOMENT.
BEOWULF'S BEARD!

WHAT'S GOING ON OUT THERE? DID YOU DOZE OFF OR SOMETHING?
OH, SNAP.
(LOSER)

AND SINCE WHEN DO YOU SAY "BINGO"? HOW DO YOU EVEN KNOW WHAT THAT IS?

I WATCH A LOT OF TV WHILE YOU'RE AT SCHOOL. I'VE GOT TO OCCUPY MYSELF SOMEHOW, YOU KNOW.

IT FELT LIKE ROGER AND I HAD REALLY FIGURED SOME THINGS OUT, AND I LEFT FEELING READY FOR ROUND TWO...

BUT AMADEUS WASN'T AT THE BUS STOP...

...OR AT LUNCH...

...OR ANYWHERE TO BE FOUND DURING RECESS.

OTHERWISE, THERE HE WAS, AT HIS DESK. BUT I COULDN'T JUST DECIDE TO INTERRUPT CLASS.
IT WOULD HAVE TO WAIT UNTIL AFTER SCHOOL.

BUT EVEN THEN, THE BELL RANG...
BRAAANG!

...AND HE WAS GONE.

HEY, E! ARE YOU GOING–?
SORRYSTEPHIE CAN'TTALK NOWGOTTA RUN...
CLEARLY, HE EXPECTED SOME KIND OF PAYBACK BECAUSE OF YESTERDAY AND HAD DECIDED TO AVOID ME.

BUT THAT WASN'T GOING TO BE EASY.
THERE ARE ONLY A FEW STREETS THAT GO FROM SCHOOL TOWARDS HIS HOUSE.

I IGNORED THOSE, OF COURSE.
HE'D TAKE A LESS OBVIOUS WAY AND THEN CIRCLE BACK.

GOTCHA.

CUTTING THROUGH THE OLD FACTORY LOT. ONCE, THEY MADE BOXED MACARONI HERE. THEN IT WAS A DRESS FACTORY. THEN A FLEA MARKET.
NOW IT'S NOTHING.

5

ROGER WAS *RIGHT.*

HE'S *GOOD.*

LED ME HERE TO *LOSE* ME...

IF I WERE *ANYONE ELSE...*

...HE
WOULD
HAVE.

HOW-?

THAT'S THE **SECOND TIME** THIS WEEK YOU'VE **SURPRISED** ME.

WHEN WAS THE **FIRST** TIME?

THAT'S FOR **ME** TO KNOW.
LET ME ASK YOU SOMETHING. IF YOU **KNOW** SO MUCH, HOW DO YOU END UP IN SO MUCH **TROUBLE** ALL THE TIME? WHY DON'T YOU JUST **AVOID** ALL THAT?
WHY **SHOULD** I?
WHAT, YOU **ENJOY IT** OR SOMETHING?

I KNOW SO MUCH **BECAUSE** OF THE TROUBLE. IT TELLS ME HOW YOU **THINK,** WHAT MAKES YOU **ANGRY,** HOW YOU'LL **REACT.**
THAT AND A LOT OF **OTHER** THINGS. NOT JUST **YOU. EVERYONE.**

LIKE WHAT **OTHER THINGS?**

LIKE HOW, OUT OF ALL THE KIDS I'VE **FOUGHT,** YOU'RE THE **ONLY ONE** THAT **HATED IT.**
MOST OF THEM FEEL **PRETTY GOOD** ABOUT THEMSELVES AFTER. **NOT YOU.**

THAT'S HARDLY AN **EXCUSE.**
I MEAN... I OWE YOU AN APOLOGY...
YEAH, **PROBABLY.** STILL, IT **TELLS** ME SOMETHING.

WHY AM I **FOLLOWING** YOU?

HA, YOU'RE ASKING **ME?**

YOU **KNOW** SO MUCH, **YOU TELL ME.**

EASY, YOU'RE MAD ABOUT YESTERDAY. DURING LUNCH.

WELL... YES AND NO...

SO? GO AHEAD. WHAT ARE YOU WAITING FOR?
WELL, HOW ABOUT THAT? I GUESS YOU DON'T KNOW EVERYTHING.
I'M NOT HERE TO FIGHT YOU, AND I'M NOT MAD THAT YOU DOUSED ME WITH ICED TEA.
I'M MAD BECAUSE I HAD IT ALL BACKWARDS AS USUAL. I'M STARTING TO THINK IT MIGHT BE A GENETIC FLAW.

EVERYONE TREATS YOU LIKE YOU'RE SOME KIND OF ***MONSTER.***

BECAUSE I ***AM.***

NO, YOU'RE NOT. BELIEVE ME, I'M AN ***EXPERT.*** I THINK YOU JUST ACT THE ONLY WAY PEOPLE WILL ***LET*** YOU.
THAT'S WHAT I ***THOUGHT.*** I'M YOUR ***PUNCHING BAG*** WHEN YOU WANT TO BE A ***HERO,*** BUT WHEN YOU FEEL ***BAD*** ABOUT IT, YOU GET TO ***SAVE ME*** FROM ***YOURSELF.***

THAT'S ***FAIR.*** BUT LIKE I SAID, I HAD IT ***BACKWARDS*** YESTERDAY.

YOU DON'T NEED ***MY*** HELP, I NEED ***YOURS.*** I CAN'T FIX THIS UNLESS ***YOU LET ME TRY...***

...STARTING WITH ***THIS:*** YOU'RE ***NOT OBLIGED*** TO BE WHAT OTHER PEOPLE ***MAKE YOU.*** IT'S ***YOUR CHOICE.***
IS IT?

IT IS.
LOOK, THIS DOESN'T HAVE TO BE COMPLICATED.

HAVE YOU NEVER HAD A FRIEND BEFORE?

...NO, WHAT FOR?

"WHAT FOR"? REALLY?
OKAY, LET'S TAKE THIS ONE STEP AT A TIME.
WE'LL WALK TO YOUR HOUSE AND YOU CAN TELL ME MORE ABOUT THOSE DR. HUMBARA COMICS.

YOU CAN'T COME INTO MY HOUSE! MY FATHER WON'T ALLOW THAT...

TAKE IT EASY, PRINCE CHARMING. I DON'T PLAN ON COMING IN.

...YOU HAVE TO STOP AT THE GATE.
FINE, WHATEVER. SO WHAT HAPPENS?
HUMBARA JUST DOES BAD STUFF AND FIGHTS THE GOOD GUYS EVERY ISSUE?

HIS ENEMY IS THE STATUS QUO...
NEVER HEARD OF HIM.

THE STATUS QUO ISN'T A "HIM," IT'S AN IDEA...

OH MAN. THIS SOUNDS BORING ALREADY. YOU KNOW ONE GOOD THING ABOUT HAVING FRIENDS IS THEY CAN LOAN YOU DECENT COMICS.

DR. HUMBARA IS A DECENT COMIC. LISTEN, DID YOU READ THE ISHTAR GAUNTLET CRISIS CROSSOVER?
EVERYONE READ THAT...
OKAY, SO THE FIRST ISSUE OF DR. HUMBARA COMES RIGHT AFTER THAT...
NO, WAIT. DIDN'T DR. HUMBARA DIE AT THE END OF THE GAUNTLET CRISIS?
NO, THAT'S WHAT EVERYBODY THOUGHT. HE ONLY APPEARED TO DIE BECAUSE IT SUITED HIS PURPOSES...

I GOT A CRASH COURSE IN EVERYTHING ***DR. HUMBARA*** HAD DONE—***AND WHY***—FROM THE END OF THE ***ISHTAR GAUNTLET CRISIS*** RIGHT UP TO THE CURRENT ISSUE, WHERE HE MATCHES WITS WITH ***ENKIDU,*** WHO HAS DONNED THE ***GILGAMESH*** MANTLE WHILE THE ***REAL*** GILGAMESH IS LOST IN THE ***MIND-MAZE*** OF ***THE PHILOSOPHER.***

THAT TOOK US RIGHT UP TO THE GATE OF THE ***HORNBURG HOUSE,*** KIND OF ON THE OUTSKIRTS OF TOWN.

IT'S NOT THAT I ***WANTED*** TO GO ANY FARTHER, BUT I HAD A ***MILLION QUESTIONS*** ABOUT HIS DAD'S ***RULE AGAINST VISITORS,*** AND I COULDN'T HELP WONDERING WHAT WOULD ***HAPPEN*** IF I PUSHED MY ***TOE,*** OR AN ***ELBOW,*** THROUGH THE GATE.

I DECIDED IT WAS BETTER TO ***TABLE*** ALL THAT FOR SOME ***OTHER DAY.*** LIKE I ALREADY SAID, ***ONE STEP AT A TIME.***

AMADEUS PROVED TRICKY TO DEAL WITH. HE WAS SUSPICIOUS AND TEMPERAMENTAL. SOMETIMES I EVEN THOUGHT HE WAS EMBARRASSED BY ME, WHICH MAKES NO SENSE!
I MEAN, I'M THE POPULAR ONE. HE'S THE OUTCAST.
BUT ALL THAT SLOWLY CHANGED. AMADEUS WAS SMART, CREATIVE, AND ACTUALLY FUNNY.
AND I CAUGHT GLIMPSES OF SOMETHING UNDERNEATH ALL THAT. HIS MOM HAD DIED JUST AFTER HE WAS BORN. HE DIDN'T REALLY REMEMBER HER AT ALL, BUT HE CARRIED HER PICTURE IN THAT LOCKET, THE ONLY THING OF HERS HE OWNED.
HE DIDN'T LIKE TO TALK ABOUT THAT, SO I DIDN'T ASK MORE, THOUGH I WANTED TO.
IN OTHER WORDS, HE WAS MOSTLY JUST LIKE A LOT OF OTHER KIDS. WE HAD JUST NEVER BOTHERED TO GET TO KNOW HIM BEFORE.
DON'T GET ME WRONG, THE KID WAS DEFINITELY STRANGE, BUT SO ARE MOST PEOPLE. ASIDE FROM THAT, I HAD STOPPED THINKING OF HIM AS SOME KIND OF MISSION.
THERE WAS SOMETHING ABOUT HIS DISCONNECT FROM ALL THE THINGS THAT WERE IMPORTANT TO OTHER KIDS THAT I REALLY RELATED TO. IT WAS HARD TO DESCRIBE, BUT IT WAS THERE.
COMMON GROUND, I GUESS YOU'D CALL IT.

MEANWHILE, I MADE SURE NO ONE LAID A FINGER ON HIM.
TAP! TAP!

THERE WASN'T A KID AT SCHOOL I COULDN'T TAKE IN A FIGHT, BUT IT NEVER CAME TO THAT.

FOR THE TRULY DEDICATED BULLIES, IT WAS AN IMPOSSIBLE SITUATION: FIGHT A GIRL AND WIN, OR (THE UNTHINKABLE) FIGHT A GIRL AND LOSE.
PRETTY SOON, THEY ALL LOST INTEREST IN EVEN TRYING.

NONE OF THIS WENT UNNOTICED.
I WAS JUST GETTING READY TO PAT MYSELF ON THE BACK AND DECLARE "MISSION ACCOMPLISHED" WHEN THINGS STARTED GOING SIDEWAYS.
LOOKING BACK, I SHOULD HAVE SEEN IT COMING.
BUT I DIDN'T.
I WALKED RIGHT INTO IT.

WE SET OUT FOR **WILLOW RIVER** AND FOLLOWED THAT NORTH.

A FEW DAYS LATER, WE HIT THE **MARSH** NO ONE HAD WARNED US ABOUT.
THERE WAS THE WAIST-DEEP **SLUDGE**, THE WAVES OF ATTACKING **STIRGES** AND **BULLYWUGS**, AND THE COVEN OF **GREEN HAGS** AT THE CENTER OF IT ALL.

WE HANDLED ALL THAT, BUT WE WERE **BOGGED DOWN** IN ENDLESS DEBATE ABOUT EVERY SINGLE MOVE WE MADE. THIS WASN'T NORMAL FOR US. WE WERE A **GREAT** TEAM, WITH SO MANY CAMPAIGNS UNDER OUR BELT WE COULD USUALLY GUESS EACH OTHER'S MOVES.

I STARTED TO THINK THEY WERE ALL **MAD** AT ME FOR SOMETHING. **ME**, NOT MY CHARACTER. BUT **THAT** DIDN'T MAKE SENSE.
DID IT?

AFTER ALMOST A WEEK ON THE ROAD, WE FINALLY REACHED **SHEEP'S EDDY**.

IT WAS NOT WHAT WE EXPECTED.
IT WAS DIRTY, DEPRESSING, AND DOWNCAST. A TOWN FULL OF PEOPLE WHO HAD GIVEN UP ON THE MOST BASIC THINGS, LIKE THEMSELVES.

WE ASKED AROUND AND WERE FINALLY SHOWN TO ISABETTA, THE TOWN MATRON. THERE SHE WAS, DOLING OUT LADLES OF THIN GRUEL TO THE STARVING TOWNSFOLK.
SHE TOOK US TO HER OFFICE AND PROCEEDED TO FILL US IN.

ONCE UPON A TIME, SHEEP'S EDDY WAS THRIVING, THANKS TO THE COPPER MINES IN THE NEARBY FOOTHILLS.
"MY HUSBAND, ORAZIO, WAS THE MASTER OF THE TOWN BY ELECTION, AND EVERYONE PROSPERED, UNTIL THE COPPER RAN OUT."
"THE PEOPLE LOOKED TO ORAZIO FOR A SOLUTION, BUT REPLACING THE TOWN'S ENTIRE INDUSTRY WASN'T GOING TO BE EASY. IT WAS A VERY DIFFICULT TIME FOR ALL OF US."

"THAT'S WHEN THE SORCERER ARRIVED, MOVING INTO THE VACATED MINES WITH AN ENTOURAGE OF EVIL CREATURES READY TO PREY UPON THE COUNTRYSIDE."

"ORAZIO, OUR SON, PRINCE, AND A GROUP OF VOLUNTEERS HEADED OUT TO CHASE THE VERMIN AWAY–"

SORRY TO INTERRUPT, BUT WHAT'S THE PRINCE'S NAME?
...
HIS NAME IS PRINCE.
YOU NAMED THE PRINCE "PRINCE"?

I THINK SHE'S SAYING "PRINCE" IS HIS NAME, NOT HIS TITLE.
OKAY, WELL... THAT POSTER WAS A LITTLE MISLEADING, THEN.

NOTED. WHERE WAS I?
AH, YES...
ORAZIO AND PRINCE MARCHED OUT TO BATTLE...
ONLY ONE MAN RETURNED. MY HUSBAND... PERISHED. AND PRINCE WAS TAKEN HOSTAGE TO ENSURE WE WOULDN'T TRY ANYTHING LIKE THAT AGAIN.

NOW WE MUST PAY TRIBUTE WITH EACH NEW MOON. THE LION'S SHARE OF ALL WE MAKE, GROW, FORAGE, SELL, OR TRADE, OR ELSE...
...NOT ONLY WOULD MY SON SUFFER, BUT OUR OWN TRIALS WOULD BECOME INFINITELY WORSE.
SO THAT'S WHY YOU PUT OUT A CALL FOR HELP.
WE'RE GOING TO RESCUE YOUR SON, ISABETTA.
AND AVENGE YOUR HUSBAND.
IT WAS NICE, FOR ONCE, TO FEEL LIKE WE WERE ALL ON THE SAME PAGE.

THE IDEA WAS TO PAY US USING THE VALUABLES THAT WOULD BE RECOVERED ONCE WE DEFEATED THE SORCERER AND HIS MINIONS.
IN THE MEANTIME, WE PROVISIONED OURSELVES AS BEST WE COULD FROM WHAT MEAGER SUPPLIES THE TOWNSFOLK HAD LEFT.
WE FELT BAD TAKING ANYTHING FROM THEM, BUT WE HAD COUNTED ON RESTOCKING AFTER THE JOURNEY HERE, AND WE COULDN'T VERY WELL ATTEMPT THE MINES WITHOUT SUPPLIES.

IN THE MORNING, WE SET OUT WITH A GUIDE WHO WOULD BRING US TO THE ENTRANCE TO THE MINES.

IT WASN'T FAR.

SOMEWHERE IN THERE WAS THE WEALTH OF THE TOWN OF SHEEP'S EDDY, THEIR CAPTIVE PRINCE WHO WASN'T REALLY A PRINCE, AND AN ARMY OF INHUMAN BRIGANDS, LED BY A SORCERER OF UNKNOWN POWER.

BUT AS WE ENTERED, I THOUGHT I SAW OUR GUIDE PULL HARD ON SOME SORT OF LEVER OUTSIDE THE ENTRANCE. WAS IT JUST A BRANCH? I DIDN'T THINK SO...

...BECAUSE A SECOND LATER, A STONE SLAB FELL INTO PLACE, TRAPPING US INSIDE THE MINE. BUT THAT WAS NOT OUR MOST IMMEDIATE CONCERN.
SLAM!
NO, THAT WOULD BE WHAT HAPPENED NEXT.

IT WAS A SETUP. AN AMBUSH. AND WE HAD WALKED RIGHT INTO IT.

THEY CAME AT US FROM ALL SIDES, THE WILDEST ASSORTMENT OF BLOODTHIRSTY BEASTS WE'D SEEN IN A LONG TIME. THERE WAS NOTHING ELSE TO DO BUT DIG IN AND FIGHT.
THE ORCS HAVE CROSSED THE RIVER! TO ARMS! TO ARMS!

DAD? WHAT ARE YOU DOING? WE STILL HAVE ANOTHER HOUR!
OH NO... I FORGOT.
YOU HAVE A DENTIST APPOINTMENT, REMEMBER?

SORRY, GUYS!
WHAT RIVER?
SOME OLD BOOK. HE'S ALWAYS QUOTING IT.

GOOD LUCK, VEEDS.
SEE YA, GUYS!

THE REST OF YOU STILL GOOD TO HANG FOR A WHILE?

NO THANKS.

UM...
OKAY?

I'M SURPRISED YOU DON'T HAVE OTHER PLANS, E.

LIKE WHAT? I THOUGHT WE'D BE PLAYING FOR A WHILE STILL.

SHE MEANS SHE'S SURPRISED YOU DON'T HAVE A DATE WITH AMADEUS.

A DATE?
I'M HANGING OUT WITH YOU RIGHT NOW.
WELL. YOU DON'T HANG OUT WITH ANYONE ELSE ANYMORE, SO...
I SEE. YOU JUST SWITCH BACK AND FORTH WHENEVER YOU WANT, RIGHT?

I...
WHAT?

I NEVER TOLD ANYONE NOT TO HANG OUT WHEN HE'S AROUND. IT SEEMS MORE LIKE YOU DON'T WANT TO.
WE DON'T.

HOW IS THAT MY FAULT? WHAT'S WRONG WITH YOU GUYS RIGHT NOW?
IT'S NOT US, E. IT'S YOU. OR IT'S HIM. WE DON'T LIKE HIM. AT ALL.

WHY? WHAT DID HE DO? YOU DON'T EVEN KNOW HIM.

WE KNOW ENOUGH.
E, LAST YEAR, YOU–

I KNOW! I KNOW! I TREATED HIM LIKE EVERYONE ELSE DOES. BUT THAT DOESN'T MAKE HIM A MONSTER, IT MAKES ME ONE.

OH GOD...
HE'S THE WEIRDEST KID AT SCHOOL. HE'S WEIRD, HIS DAD'S WEIRD, THEIR HOUSE IS WEIRD, EVERYONE KNOWS IT.

SO WHAT?

E, I'M ASKING YOU, YES OR NO, ARE YOU GOING TO KEEP HANGING OUT WITH HIM?

YES! CAN YOU GUYS JUST GIVE HIM A CHANCE?

NO.

NO.

NO.

C'MON, GUYS!
HE'S JUST ANOTHER KID, LIKE US.
HE LIKES... COMICS.
HE LIKES TO DRAW.
I KNOW HE'S A WEIRDO.
AREN'T WE ALL WEIRDOS?

I HAVE TO GO.
ME TOO.
WHO WANTS HOT DOGS?

BYE, MRS. WEGMUND...
OH, YOU GUYS ARE DONE SO EARLY...

PHOEBE, EOWULF, HOT DOGS?

NO THANK YOU, MRS. WEGMUND. I HAVE TO GO, TOO.

I NEED THE RESTROOM FIRST, THOUGH...
YOU KNOW WHERE IT IS!

DID SOMEBODY *DIE?*

I'M NOT SURE.

WELL, REMEMBER, IT'S JUST A *GAME,* SWEETIE.
TRUE.
BUT I HAD GOTTEN MY *WISH.* WHATEVER *DELICATE BARRIERS* SEPARATED *GAME MODE* FROM *JERSEY MODE* FROM WHAT I CALLED *ADVENTURE MODE* HAD STARTED TO *DISSOLVE.*
EVERYTHING WAS BECOMING *EVERYTHING ELSE.*

2
SECRET
DOORS.

RAAAAAAA!

I'VE BEEN LOOKING ALL OVER FOR YOU. WHERE'D YOU GET ALL THAT STUFF?

IT TOOK A WHILE TO PUT ALL THIS ON.
IT WAS IN THE ROOM WITH ALL THE MAPS...

YEAH, I CALL THAT THE MAP ROOM. WE'RE REALLY NOT SUPPOSED TO BE IN THERE...
HA! TAKE THAT!
OH, SORRY. BUT WHAT ABOUT THOSE MAPS?
THEY'RE NOT REAL, ARE THEY?

NOT UNLESS YOU BELIEVE SOMEONE MADE A REAL MAP OF HADES.
HM. I DON'T KNOW. I MIGHT.

ANYWAY, LET'S PUT ALL THAT BACK. MY DAD'S A REAL NERD ABOUT HIS COLLECTIBLES...

DON'T WORRY, MY DAD'S THE **SAME.**

OH YEAH? WHAT DOES **HE** COLLECT?

WEIRD STUFF. I DON'T KNOW WHAT HALF OF IT IS.

THERE. PERFECT.

KLANK!

LOOKS LIKE IT'S SUPPOSED TO LOCK ON TO THOSE **TABS.**
WHAT DO YOU THINK I'M **TRYING** TO DO?

THERE!

KLANK!

HERE, LET ME TRY...
NO, I'LL GET IT...

I THINK YOU'VE GOT TO **PUSH DOWN** ON IT HARDER...
NO, IT HAS TO **TWIST** A LITTLE **THIS WAY...**

CRINK!
WHOOPS!
WHOA!

SWISH!

UH... YOU *KNEW* ABOUT THAT, RIGHT?
...YEAH!
OF *COURSE* I DID!
NO, I DIDN'T!
HOW IS THAT *POSSIBLE?*

WELL...
WHERE'S IT *GO?*
WAIT!

WE'RE NOT ALLOWED!
WE'RE NOT ALLOWED TO LOOK?
YOUR DAD'S GOT MORE RULES THAN MINE!
YEAH, WELL, THAT'S HOW IT IS!
WHAT'VE YOU GOT DOWN THERE? RADIOACTIVE SKELETONS?

NO–I MEAN YES! THAT'S IT!
IT'S AN OLD FALLOUT SHELTER!
PREVIOUS OWNER MADE IT.
SNAP!

YOU KNOW, A REAL CRACKPOT!
FALLOUT SHELTERS AREN'T THAT STRANGE. WHY CAN'T WE SEE IT?

UH...BECAUSE... THE RATS! TERRIBLE RAT PROBLEM DOWN THERE!
NOW WE'VE GOT TO GET THIS DOOR CLOSED BEFORE ANY GET UP HERE!

KRANK!
SHUT!
YES!
EOWULF?

MOM! HI!
WHAT ARE YOU–?
OH, I DIDN'T KNOW YOU HAD A FRIEND OVER...

YES! THIS IS MY FRIEND AMADEUS!
HI.

NOT...
AMADEUS HORNBURG?

YES, MA'AM.
THAT'S ME.

EOWULF, MAKE SURE THAT MESS GETS PICKED UP...
AND THEN YOU AND I NEED TO TALK. I'M SURE YOUR FRIEND WILL UNDERSTAND.

I GUESS THAT'S MY CUE TO *LEAVE.*
SEE YOU TOMORROW...

DON'T BOTHER.
HUH? WHAT'S *THAT* SUPPOSED TO MEAN?

YOU SAW WHAT *HAPPENED* WHEN SHE FIGURED OUT *WHO I WAS.*
I'M NOT STUPID!
WHAT? NO, *NO!* THAT'S... THAT'S NOT-

SORRY IF I GOT YOU IN *TROUBLE.*
AT LEAST NOW YOU *KNOW*–TO *SOME* PEOPLE, A *MONSTER* IS ALL I'LL *EVER* BE.
YOU *DIDN'T...*

TARU'S TORRENTS!
AMADEUS HORNBURG? *REALLY?*

WHY DID YOU **DO THAT?** HE **ALREADY** THINKS EVERYONE **HATES** HIM.

I KNOW YOU DON'T LIKE BEING **BACK,** BUT IF BRINGING THAT BOY HERE IS YOUR IDEA OF **ACTING OUT,** YOU AND I ARE GOING TO HAVE **TROUBLE.**

I'M **NOT** ACTING OUT!
THE **HORNBURGS** ARE ALWAYS UP TO **SOMETHING.** YOU HAVE TO KEEP AN **EYE** ON THEM, ESPECIALLY IN **THIS** HOUSE. THEY'RE NOT **LIKE** EVERYONE ELSE.

NEITHER ARE **WE.**

YOU **KNOW** WHAT I MEAN.

I **DON'T** KNOW. HE WASN'T **UP** TO ANYTHING, MOM. WE WERE JUST–

DON'T BRING HIM HERE AGAIN. IS THAT **CLEAR?**

WHY?
WHAT'S GOING ON?

EOWULF WAS IN THE *MAP ROOM...*
OKAY, THAT'S *NOT* A BIG DEAL–
WITH THE *HORNBURG* BOY.

OH... SIGH... I WAS *AFRAID* THINGS WERE HEADED THIS WAY...
YOU WERE–?

YOU MEAN YOU *KNEW* ABOUT THIS?
I HEARD A *RUMOR.*

FROM *WHO?* ARE YOU GUYS *SPYING* ON ME?
NOBODY'S *SPYING.*
IF YOU *KNEW,* WHY DIDN'T YOU *SAY* SOMETHING?

I GUESS BECAUSE I *TRUSTED* EOWULF COULD HANDLE IT.

YOU TRUSTED HER? YOUR JOB IS TO PROTECT HER!
PROTECT ME FROM WHAT? HE'S NOT SOME KIND OF WILD ANIMAL, YOU KNOW! IF THERE'S A REASON I SHOULD STAY AWAY FROM HIM, WHAT IS IT?

RIGHT. HOW MANY SECRETS ARE YOU KEEPING FROM ME?

E, WE'RE NOT KEEPING SECRETS–

THAT'S A LIE!

GO TO YOUR ROOM.
NOW!

DAD, HE'S *NOT* A MONSTER...

JUST...
DO WHAT YOUR MOM SAYS, *E.*

FINE.

BUT THIS ISN'T *OVER.*

OH, YOU CAN *BET* ON *THAT!*

ROGER WAS *RIGHT.* I HAVE *NO IDEA* WHO *YOU TWO* EVEN *ARE.*

I MUST HAVE FALLEN ASLEEP READING COMICS AND COMPLAINING TO ROGER ABOUT EVERYTHING: AMADEUS, MY PARENTS, A SECRET DOOR THAT WAS SOMEHOW SECRET EVEN FROM ME.
ROGER WAS NOW CONVINCED MY "REAL PARENTS" HAD BEEN REPLACED BY SHAPE-SHIFTERS.
HE'S PRETTY SMART FOR A SWORD, BUT THERE'S A LOT ABOUT PARENTS HE DOESN'T GET, AND I WAS STILL PRETTY SURE THESE WERE THE REAL DEAL.
AS PARENTS GO, MINE WERE NOT NORMAL. BUT EVERY SO OFTEN THEY COULD STILL SURPRISE ME WITH SOME VERY TYPICAL PARENT BEHAVIOR. WHAT IT PROVED WAS THAT THEY WERE HIDING SOMETHING.
SOMETHING BIG.

I ALREADY KNOW I'M DESCENDED FROM BEOWULF IN A LONG, UNBROKEN LINE OF MONSTER HUNTERS, I'VE TRAVELED TO OTHER DIMENSIONS, PARTIED WITH UNICORNS, FOUGHT EVIL GODS, ETC.
I MEAN, WHAT ELSE IS THERE TO HIDE, RIGHT?

THE ANSWER WAS ON THE WAY, BUT NOT BEFORE THOSE BARRIERS I MENTIONED EARLIER COMPLETELY COLLAPSED.
WHU-?
RRRRUUMBBLE!

WHAT IN THE WIDE WORLD OF SPORTS IS HAPPENING?
FEELS LIKE AN EARTH-QUAKE!

RROAARRR!
E, LOOK OUTSIDE!

RRRAAAAAAH!
BEOWULF'S BEARD!
A MONSTER! BUT NOT IN SOME FAR-OFF REALM OR DIMENSION. IT WAS RIGHT THERE, PLAIN AS DAY, ON MY OWN FRONT LAWN!
HOW?
WHY???

THIS CAN'T HAPPEN HERE– IT'S ADVENTURE MODE STUFF!
KLICK <WHIR> "FORGET NEW JERSEY, FORGET SCHOOL. IT'S THE SAME AS ANY OTHER REALM OR DIMENSION WE'VE BEEN THROUGH."
YOU RECORDED ME?
YES!
WELL– I TAKE IT BACK!
TELL IT TO THE WORM!

WE'VE GOTTA GET OUT THERE AND DO SOMETHING!
HELMET? SHIELD?
SOCKS?

NO TIME FOR THAT-!

WHAT THE-?
SQUISH!
KLATTER!

WAM!

GRENDEL'S GRAPPLERS- WHAT WAS THAT?!
THANKS FOR TELLING ME!
YOU WERE ASLEEP, SO YOUR MOM LEFT YOU SOME DINNER...
WELL, I'M SORRY! THE GIANT WORM ATTACKING YOUR BLOCK SEEMED MORE IMPORTANT!

IT IS, I JUST DIDN'T EXPECT TO GET AMBUSHED BY LEFTOVERS!
I WON'T BE MUCH HELP OUTSIDE IF I'M KNOCKED SENSELESS BY A PLATE OF MEAT LOAF!

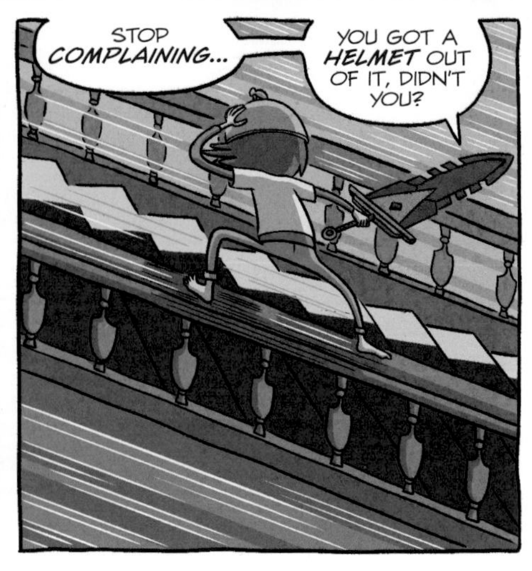
STOP COMPLAINING...
YOU GOT A HELMET OUT OF IT, DIDN'T YOU?

LOOKS LIKE SOMEONE BEAT US HERE!

DAD?
STAY INSIDE, E. I'VE GOT THIS.

SORRY, DAD. NOT A CHANCE!

WELL, THEN AT LEAST TRY TO FOLLOW MY LEAD, OKAY?

WAAA!
UH...I'LL DO MY BEST!
GRAB!

ROGER?
BORN READY, *ETC.*

KRA-BOOM!
WHOA! HOW'D YOU *DO* THAT?
WASN'T ME-

-LOOK!

FLING!

SHING!

SHANG!

HAHA! THANKS, QUEEN MANTIS!
RRRAAAAAAAH!
CHOP!

"QUEEN MANTIS"? ROG, DID YOU HEAR THAT?
I DID!
BUT THAT MEANS...
RROAARRR!

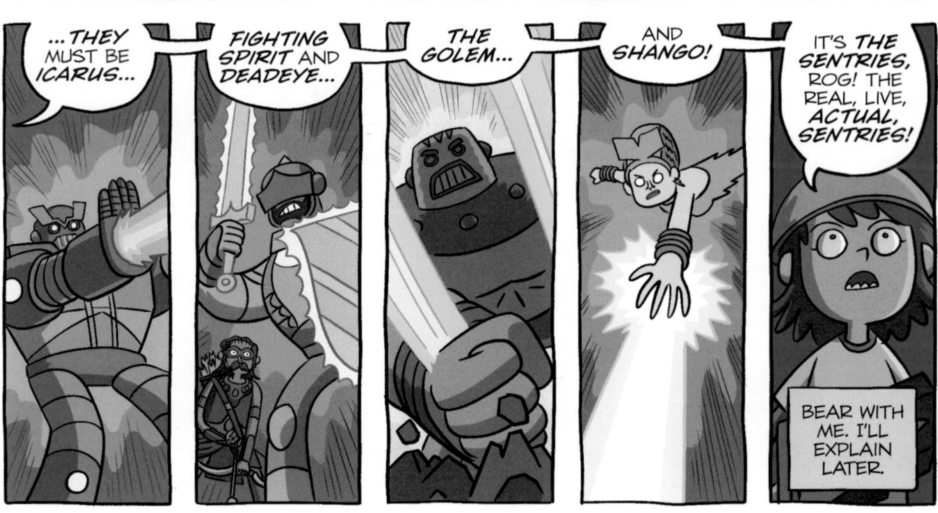
...THEY MUST BE ICARUS...
FIGHTING SPIRIT AND DEADEYE...
THE GOLEM...
AND SHANGO!
IT'S THE SENTRIES, ROG! THE REAL, LIVE, ACTUAL, SENTRIES!
BEAR WITH ME. I'LL EXPLAIN LATER.

ZRAKKA!
KRA-ZOW!
ZAM!
THE SENTRIES ARE A SOCIAL MEDIA MYTH. THEY DON'T EXIST!
TELL THAT TO THE WORM!

GREAT WORK, SENTRIES! THE MONSTER'S IN FULL RETREAT!
DAD!

YOU KNOW THE SENTRIES? I CAN'T BELIEVE THEY'RE REALLY REAL! AND THEY'RE ALL HERE!
I MEAN... EXCEPT FOR THE GUY THEY CALLED...

...GREAT HERDS OF HOWLING HARPIES!

MY DAD IS THE BERSERKER!!! HEY, THAT'S NOT YOUR REAL COSTUME, IS IT?
HUH? NO–! I WAS ALREADY IN BED AND THERE WAS NO TIME TO–
GUESS THAT MONSTER CAUGHT YOU ON LAUNDRY DAY, HUH, BIG B?
GET A LOAD OF THE KID! WHERE'D YOU FIND THAT HELMET, THE PANTRY?
DON'T MAKE FUN, SPIRIT– THE KID'S GOT MOXIE!

HEADS UP, TEAM– WE'VE GOT TO DEAL WITH THESE CIVILIANS...

ON IT!
WHAT'S HE GOING TO DO?
JUST WATCH...

ALL RIGHT, EVERYONE– IF YOU'LL JUST GATHER 'ROUND AND DIRECT YOUR ATTENTION TO THE ACCLIMATOR HERE ON MY CHEST PLATE...

FLASH!
OKAY, EVERYONE! NOTHING TO SEE HERE! LET'S ALL GO HOME NOW!

I DON'T GET IT. WHAT JUST HAPPENED?
STANDARD MEMORY WIPE TECHNOLOGY. ICARUS IS A WIZ AT THAT STUFF! WHEN THEY WAKE UP TOMORROW, THEY WON'T REMEMBER US OR ANY OF THIS!

WHAT ABOUT THE GIANT HOLE?
ICARUS' DRONES WILL DO ENOUGH TERRAFORMING TO MAKE IT LOOK LIKE A NATURAL SINKHOLE!
PFFT!
PFFT!

SO THAT'S WHY EVERYONE THINKS THE SENTRIES ARE JUST A MYTH-YOU'RE TOO GOOD AT COVERING YOUR TRACKS!
HEY-! ARE THEY ALL COMING TO OUR HOUSE?

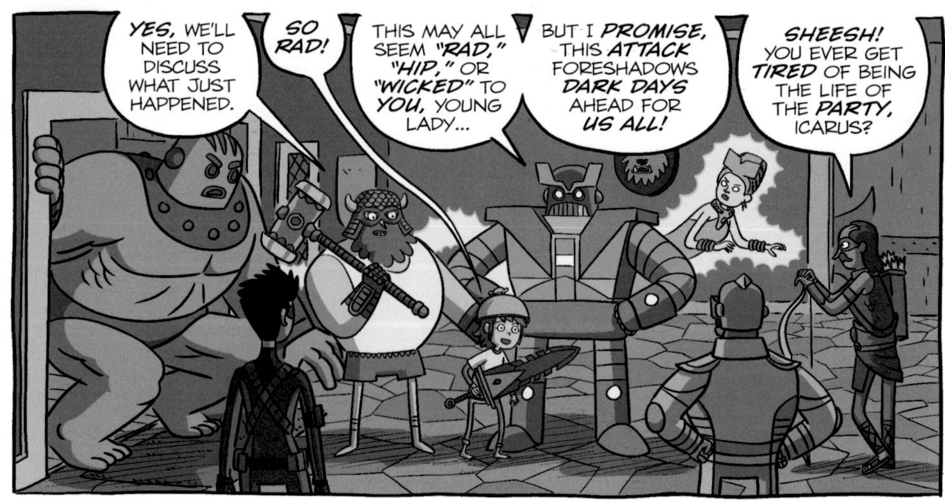
YES, WE'LL NEED TO DISCUSS WHAT JUST HAPPENED.
SO RAD!
THIS MAY ALL SEEM "RAD," "HIP," OR "WICKED" TO YOU, YOUNG LADY...
BUT I PROMISE, THIS ATTACK FORESHADOWS DARK DAYS AHEAD FOR US ALL!
SHEESH! YOU EVER GET TIRED OF BEING THE LIFE OF THE PARTY, ICARUS?

ALL RIGHT, I KNOW IT'S BEEN A WHILE, BUT YOU ALL KNOW THE WAY...
WAIT, THEY'VE BEEN HERE BEFORE?

E, I'M GOING TO NEED YOU TO GO BACK TO YOUR ROOM NOW.
WHAT?

NO, I WANT TO HANG OUT WITH YOU GUYS!

IT'S NOT A HANGOUT, E. WE'VE GOT SERIOUS THINGS TO DISCUSS.

I AM SERIOUS!
SHUT!

ROGER, CAN YOU HEAR WHAT'S GOING ON IN THERE?
HOLD ON, SCANNING THE ROOM...
AHEM!

MOM! ...DIDN'T SEE YOU THERE...
WHAT A NIGHT, HUH?
DID YOU KNOW DAD WAS A SUPERHERO?

ARE YOU A SUPERHERO?

I DON'T REMEMBER GIVING YOU PERMISSION TO LEAVE YOUR ROOM.
WHA-? REALLY? WE WERE JUST ATTACKED BY A GIANT WORM! C'MON!
UPSTAIRS. NOW.

AW, MOM...
GO!

HOW'D WE DO?
YOU'RE A CHAMPION STALLER. I WAS ABLE TO SCAN A FEW FREQUENCIES AND SPECTRUMS-

AND?
AND NOTHING...
HOW IS THAT POSSIBLE? YOU'RE TELLING ME THAT ROOM IS SOUNDPROOF? INFRARED-PROOF?
NO, NEITHER- I'M TELLING YOU THE ROOM WAS EMPTY!

SCRAPE!

OF COURSE! THE SECRET DOOR!
SNAP!

ROGER, THERE MUST BE SOME KIND OF MEETING ROOM OR—WHO KNOWS?—A WHOLE SECRET HEADQUARTERS BACK THERE! EVERY SUPERHERO GROUP HAS ONE!

WE'VE GOT TO FIND OUT WHAT'S BEHIND THAT BOOKCASE!
AGREED, BUT WE'VE GOT TO BE SMART ABOUT IT OR WE'LL GET CAUGHT.

OF COURSE WE'LL BE SMART! WHEN ARE WE NOT SMART? AREN'T WE ALWAYS SMART?
YOU MEAN "WE" GOT CAUGHT...
NO. THERE WAS THAT TIME YOU GOT CAUGHT BY TYPHON...

...THE TIME YOU TELEPORTED US TO THE MIDDLE OF THE OCEAN...
TECHNICALLY, THAT WAS A SEA...

YOU LET MY BATTERY DIE DURING BATTLE. TWICE.
C'MON, BUDDY. IT'S YOUR BATTERY. YOU DON'T SEE MY BATTERY DYING, DO YOU?

LOOK, I GET YOUR POINT. WE'LL WAIT UNTIL MOM AND DAD ARE ASLEEP, AND THEN-

OBVIOUSLY, BUT NOT TONIGHT!
WHY NOT? WHAT'VE YOU GOT, A DATE?
WE SHOULD WAIT UNTIL THINGS COOL DOWN A BIT. EVERYONE'S VERY KEYED UP RIGHT NOW.
LET'S GIVE IT A FEW DAYS, AT LEAST.

FINE, YOU WIN, WE'LL WAIT.
LISTEN, I'VE BEEN THINKING...
...SINCE ADVENTURE MODE HAS CLEARLY CROSSED OVER INTO JERSEY MODE, I THINK WE SHOULD START ACTING LIKE IT...
SPEAK FOR YOURSELF.

I AM. ANYTHING CAN HAPPEN AT ANY TIME. I'M GOING TO NEED MY GEAR ON ME.
THE BOTTOMLESS BACKPACK—GOOD THINKING! BUT YOU ALREADY FORGOT SOMETHING...

WHAT'S THAT?
ME! IN A TIGHT SPOT, I'M WORTH TWICE THE REST OF THAT STUFF!

YEAH, BUT MOM SAID–
I KNOW, BUT ARE WE ON A MISSION OR NOT?

YOU'RE ASKING ME TO DISOBEY A DIRECT ORDER.

I'M ASKING YOU TO PLAY THIS SMART. IF YOU DON'T NEED ME, I STAY IN THE BACKPACK.
NOK! NOK!

HEY, KIDDO...

...
OH, HEY.
RAN OUT OF SERIOUS THINGS TO DISCUSS?
DROP!

NO, ACTUALLY. WE NEED TO TALK ABOUT SOME STUFF...
WHAT, AGAIN?

OKAY, OKAY.
WHAT IS IT THIS TIME?

I NEED YOU TO TRY AND REMEMBER **HOW LONG** AMADEUS WAS BY HIMSELF IN THE HOUSE.
REALLY? THAT'S WHAT YOU WANT TO TALK ABOUT?
IT'S **IMPORTANT.**

WHY?

WHY DOES **EVERY** CONVERSATION FEEL LIKE AN **ARGUMENT** LATELY? WHAT'S **GOING ON** WITH US?

THAT'S WHAT **I'D** LIKE TO KNOW. YOU **USED** TO TRUST ME.

WE **DO** TRUST YOU.

NO, YOU DON'T!

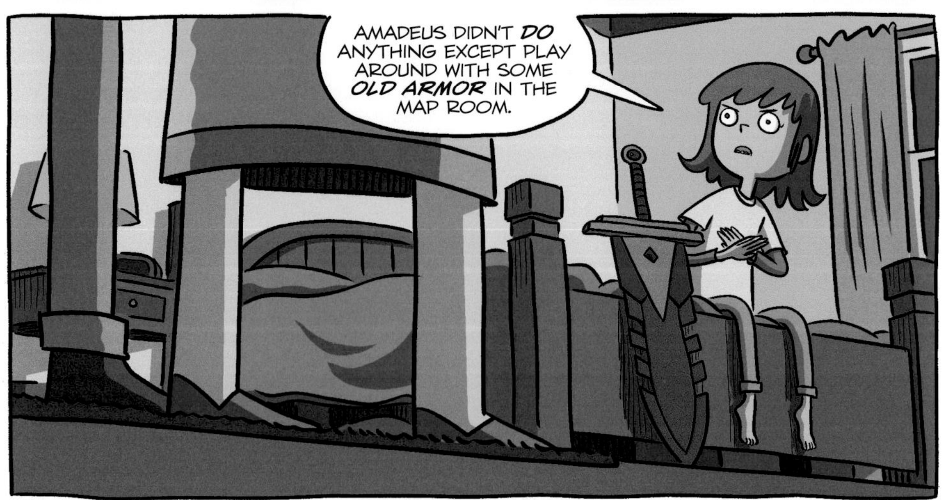
AMADEUS DIDN'T **DO** ANYTHING EXCEPT PLAY AROUND WITH SOME **OLD ARMOR** IN THE MAP ROOM.

WHICH ARMOR?

...

TRUST WORKS BOTH WAYS, YOU KNOW.

...SIGH...

...THE RED ONE.

ARE YOU TRYING TO SAY HE HAD SOMETHING TO DO WITH THAT WORM? YOU KNOW HOW CRAZY THAT SOUNDS? HE'S A KID.
SO ARE YOU.
NO ONE'S ACCUSING HIM OF ANYTHING. WE DON'T KNOW WHAT HAPPENED. WE'RE STILL TRYING TO FIGURE IT OUT.

WELL, THEN SO WHAT IF HE WAS ALONE IN THE MAP ROOM? IT'S JUST MAPS, RIGHT?

RIGHT?

HOW LONG?

I DON'T KNOW. I DIDN'T TIME HIM.

TAKE A GUESS.

I DON'T KNOW.

E, THIS IS NOT HELPING YOUR FRIEND. YOU COULD PUT HIM IN THE CLEAR RIGHT NOW BY JUST ANSWERING THE QUESTION. OTHERWISE, WE HAVE TO TAKE OTHER STEPS.
WHAT'S THAT MEAN?

CAN YOU GUESS APPROXIMATELY HOW LONG HE WAS ALONE?
NO.

YOU CAN'T, OR YOU WON'T?

BOTH.

OKAY, OKAY! I DO ADMIRE YOUR LOYALTY TO SOMEONE YOU THINK IS YOUR FRIEND–

HE IS MY FRIEND!

I REALLY HOPE SO. HAVE A GOOD NIGHT, E.
HOW LONG AM I STUCK IN THIS ROOM?

WE'LL LET YOU KNOW.
HE DIDN'T DO ANYTHING!

NEITHER DID I.
BUT I COULDN'T ASK HIM MYSELF. AMADEUS WASN'T AT SCHOOL THE NEXT DAY...

...OR THE NEXT...

...OR THE NEXT.

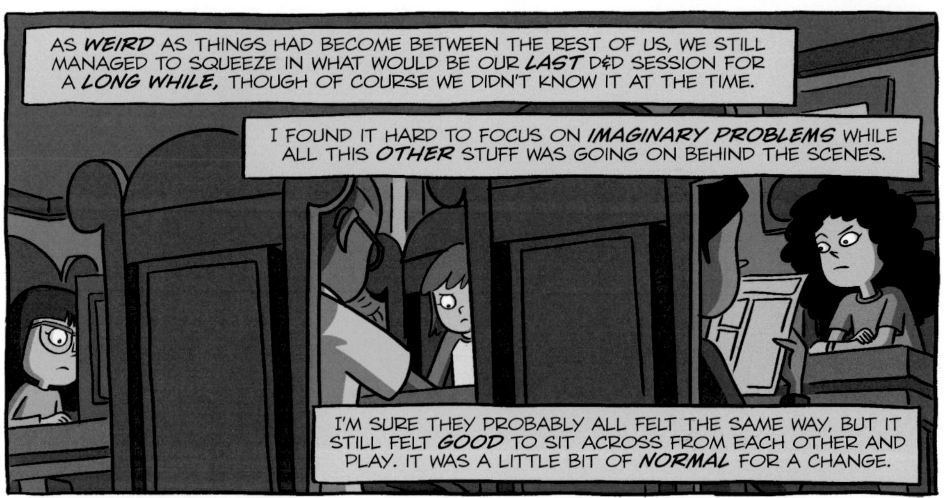
AS WEIRD AS THINGS HAD BECOME BETWEEN THE REST OF US, WE STILL MANAGED TO SQUEEZE IN WHAT WOULD BE OUR LAST D&D SESSION FOR A LONG WHILE, THOUGH OF COURSE WE DIDN'T KNOW IT AT THE TIME.
I FOUND IT HARD TO FOCUS ON IMAGINARY PROBLEMS WHILE ALL THIS OTHER STUFF WAS GOING ON BEHIND THE SCENES.
I'M SURE THEY PROBABLY ALL FELT THE SAME WAY, BUT IT STILL FELT GOOD TO SIT ACROSS FROM EACH OTHER AND PLAY. IT WAS A LITTLE BIT OF NORMAL FOR A CHANGE.

WE SURVIVED THAT FIRST AMBUSH, AND FROM THAT POINT ON, IT WAS A BLUR OF HIT-AND-RUN ATTACKS BY THE MINE'S DENIZENS.
WE WERE ABLE TO FIGHT EACH OF THOSE OFF, BUT IT WAS BEGINNING TO TAKE ITS TOLL.

FINALLY, STEPHIE WAS DOWN AND VEDA'S FLAMING SPHERE WAS THE ONLY THING THAT ALLOWED US TO ESCAPE.

THEN, WE WERE RUNNING BLIND, NO LONGER MAPPING OUR WAY THROUGH, NO IDEA HOW TO GO BACK, NO IDEA WHERE WE WERE HEADING.

WE JUST NEEDED A BREAK FROM THE CONSTANT ATTACKS. A CHANCE TO CATCH OUR BREATH AND REGAIN OUR STRENGTH.

INSTEAD, WE RAN FULL SPEED INTO AN ENORMOUS DIRE WOLF. MY GAME VERSION OF ROGER MADE SHORT WORK OF IT, AND IT WAS ONLY AFTERWARDS THAT WE REALIZED WHAT IT WAS GUARDING...

WE HAD FOUND PRINCE.

HE WAS A LITTLE WORSE FOR WEAR, BUT HE'D LIVE IF WE COULD MAKE IT OUT ALIVE.

A SWIG OF ELIXIR AND A HEALING SPELL LATER, AND THIS IS WHAT HE TOLD US...

LIKE ISABETTA SAID, PRINCE, ORAZIO, AND HIS HANDPICKED MEN MARCHED OUT FROM SHEEP'S EDDY, BUT THERE HAD BEEN NO BATTLE.
THEY HAD MET WITH THE BANDITS AND THEIR LEADER IN A GLADE NEAR THE MINE'S ENTRANCE. IT HAD ALL BEEN PREARRANGED.

THE BANDIT LEADER HAD A PROPOSITION. SINCE THERE WAS NO MORE WEALTH TO DIG OUT OF THE MINES, WHAT IF THERE WAS A WAY TO POUR WEALTH INTO IT, AND THEN DIVIDE IT EQUALLY BETWEEN THEMSELVES?

THE BANDITS IN THE MINES WOULD PLAY THE EVIL OUTLAWS...
...AND THE TOWNSFOLK WOULD BE THE HAPLESS VICTIMS, SENDING OUT A DESPERATE PLEA FOR AID.

THOSE WHO ANSWERED THE CALL, ADVENTURERS AND HARDENED CAMPAIGNERS, WOULD BRING WITH THEM COSTLY ARMOR, PRICELESS ENCHANTED WEAPONS, AMULETS, TRINKETS, GEAR, AND OTHER TREASURES THEY'D FOUND IN FOREIGN LANDS. THE BANDITS ONLY HAD TO DO AWAY WITH THEM IN THE DARK OF THE MINES, AND THESE VALUABLES WOULD BE RIPE FOR THE PICKING.

IT WAS INGENIOUS AND INSIDIOUS, BUT, FROM ORAZIO'S POINT OF VIEW, IT WOULD KEEP THE BANDITS BUSY AND THE TOWN OF SHEEP'S EDDY ALIVE, AND THAT WAS GOOD ENOUGH FOR HIM. PRINCE WAS THE ONLY ONE TO OBJECT.

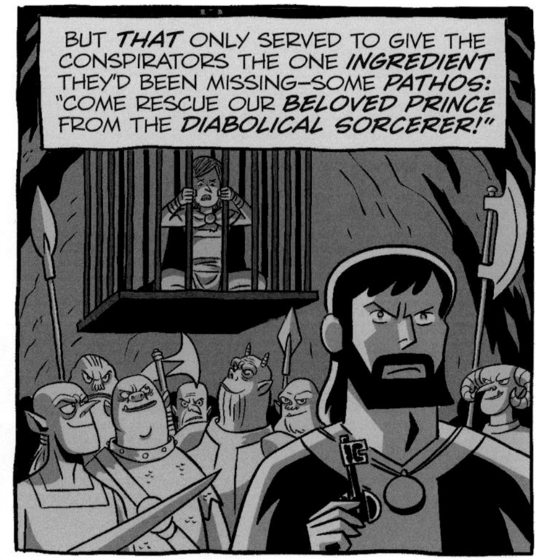
BUT THAT ONLY SERVED TO GIVE THE CONSPIRATORS THE ONE INGREDIENT THEY'D BEEN MISSING—SOME PATHOS: "COME RESCUE OUR BELOVED PRINCE FROM THE DIABOLICAL SORCERER!"

WHAT ABOUT THAT SORCERER? DOES HE EVEN EXIST?
AND WHAT ABOUT ORAZIO, YOUR DAD? ISABETTA TOLD US HE WAS DEAD.

DEAD? HE'S DEAD TO ME, THAT'S FOR SURE!
MY FATHER IS THE ONE THEY CALL THE SORCERER, BUT HE HAS NO REAL MAGIC, ONLY LIES!

THANKS FOR FREEING ME FROM THAT CAGE, BUT THERE'S NO RESCUING ME FROM THIS TRUTH...
NOTHING YOU'VE DONE HERE MATTERS IF WE DON'T PUT A STOP TO ALL THIS!

THE BANDITS, THE TOWNSFOLK, MY PARENTS—THEY'RE ALL IN ON IT, AND THEY'RE ALL THE SAME! THEY MUST BE PUNISHED! THEY ALL HAVE TO PAY FOR WHAT THEY'VE DONE!
TSK! TSK!

MY SON HAS ALWAYS BEEN SO DRAMATIC!

THE WORLD IS JUST NOT AS SIMPLISTIC, NOT AS BLACK-AND-WHITE, AS YOU WANT IT TO BE, PRINCE.
YOU MIGHT HAVE LEARNED THAT SOMEDAY, IF YOU HAD LIVED LONG ENOUGH TO GROW UP!
I THINK WE MADE YOUR DAD ANGRY...
WHAT A CLIFF-HANGER, RIGHT? PHOEBE REALLY IS A GREAT DM. I DON'T KNOW HOW SHE THINKS OF ALL THIS STUFF.
BUT THAT'S AS FAR AS WE GOT. LOOKING BACK, IT WOULD PROVE TO BE JUST FAR ENOUGH.

MEANWHILE, AMADEUS WAS **M.I.A.**
THE LONGER IT WENT ON, THE MORE I STARTED TO **WONDER.**

AND I **HATED** THAT.
I KNOW SO MUCH **BECAUSE** OF THE TROUBLE. IT TELLS ME HOW YOU **THINK,** WHAT MAKES YOU **ANGRY,** HOW YOU'LL **REACT.**
COULD AMADEUS HAVE BEEN **STEERING** THINGS THE **WHOLE TIME?**

DID HE **USE** ME JUST TO GET INTO THE **HOUSE?**
DID HE ALREADY **KNOW** SOMETHING ABOUT US?

OR ABOUT THE **STUFF** WE HAD LYING AROUND?
OR THE **BOOKCASE** IN THE MAP ROOM?

PHOEBE, VEDA, LANCE, STEPHIE, MOM, DAD—WERE ALL OF THEM RIGHT ABOUT HIM ALL ALONG? HECK, EVEN ROGER TRIED TO WARN ME.
COULD I HAVE BEEN THAT STUPID?

I DIDN'T KNOW ABOUT THE SECRET DOOR. I DIDN'T KNOW ABOUT MY DAD. WHAT ELSE DIDN'T I KNOW?
AND THE QUESTION THAT REALLY MADE MY SKIN CRAWL: WHAT DID EVERYONE ELSE KNOW THAT I DIDN'T KNOW THEY KNEW?

I HADN'T FORGOTTEN ABOUT THAT BOOKCASE BY A LONG SHOT. THERE WERE ANSWERS BACK THERE FOR SURE. BUT THERE WERE OTHER ANSWERS IN OTHER PLACES, AND I NEEDED THOSE FIRST.

I WASN'T UNDER HOUSE ARREST ANYMORE, BUT "HEY, MOM! I'M JUST GOING TO POP BY THE HORNBURGS' FOR A BIT" WOULD NEVER FLY.

I DON'T LIKE SNEAKING AROUND. IT'S NOT MY STYLE, BUT I DIDN'T HAVE ANY OTHER CHOICE.
THE WHOLE THING HINGED ON THE ONLY PERSON I COULD STILL TRUST...

LET ME HEAR IT ONE MORE TIME...

NOW?
YES!

SIGH...
KLICK <WHIR>
"SNORE! SNOOORRE! SNORE!"

THAT'S AMAZING! IT REALLY SOUNDS LIKE ME!
IT IS YOU. I WAS RECORDING ALL NIGHT.

YOU'RE A TROUPER.

OKAY, *HIT* ME.
YES, YES, *HURRY UP* ALREADY!
YOU'RE *SURE* ABOUT THIS?

OKAY. YOU *ASKED* FOR IT...
KRR-ZAK!

TARU'S TORRENTS, TAKE IT *EASY!*
I *DID.* THAT WAS MY *LOWEST* SETTING.

REMIND ME NOT TO GET ON YOUR *BAD SIDE...*

...HEY MOM...
HI–
ARE YOU OKAY?

ME? YEAH... JUST A LITTLE BUSHED I GUESS...
YOU LOOK FLUSHED...
AND YOU'RE VERY WARM. YOU MIGHT BE COMING DOWN WITH SOMETHING.

MM. I'LL BE OKAY. THINK I'LL JUST HIT THE SACK. REALLY TIRED...
GOOD IDEA. I'LL COME UP AND CHECK ON YOU LATER.

'KAY, MOM. BUT IF I'M SLEEPING, DON'T WAKE ME. REALLY TIRED...

SO FAR, SO GOOD, PARTNER!

I HAVE MISGIVINGS ABOUT THIS CAPER.
WHY? IT'LL BE JUST LIKE STORMING AHRIMAN'S HEADQUARTERS.

THAT WAS A TERRIBLE PLAN! YOU ALMOST DIED, AND THIS TIME YOU WON'T HAVE ME THERE TO SAVE YOU.

I NEED YOU HERE TO COVER FOR ME IN CASE MOM OR DAD COME IN.

BESIDES, THIS ISN'T A FIGHT. I'M JUST TRYING TO GET SOME ANSWERS.
CAN I COUNT ON YOU OR NOT?
OTHERS MAY NOT SEE IT THAT WAY.

YOU KNOW THE ANSWER TO THAT.
GOOD!

OPERATION: HOUSE CALL! HERE WE GO...!
THE PLAN WAS TO JUST SHIFT RIGHT INSIDE AMADEUS' HOUSE. IT WAS RISKY, SURE. BUT DESPERATE TIMES CALL FOR DESPERATE MEASURES.

OOOF!
IT WAS LIKE WALKING INTO A BRICK WALL MADE OUT OF ELECTRIC BRICKS.

THERE WAS SOME KIND OF PROTECTION AROUND THE WHOLE PLACE. I'D NEVER FELT ANYTHING LIKE IT. I THOUGHT ABOUT SCRUBBING THE MISSION THEN AND THERE, BEFORE SOMEONE SAW ME. BUT LIKE I SAID, I NEEDED ANSWERS.

PLUS, I HAD A ***PLAN B...***

IF YOU OWN A CLOAK OF INVISIBILITY...**USE IT!**

BING!
BONG!

SNEAK!
SNEAK!
SNEAK!

IVOR?

WHO'S AT THE DOOR, MAN?

SO THAT WAS MR. HORNBURG. I'M NOT SURE WHAT I WAS EXPECTING, BUT I COULDN'T IMAGINE SOMEONE MORE DIFFERENT FROM AMADEUS.
THERE'S NO ONE, SIR!
NO ONE? NONSENSE! DOORBELLS DON'T RING THEMSELVES!

AMADEUS' HOUSE DEFINITELY HAD A LOT OF... CHARACTER. BUT I GUESS MY PLACE WAS PRETTY WEIRD BY NORMAL STANDARDS, TOO.

AMADEUS SAID HE DIDN'T KNOW WHAT HALF THIS STUFF EVEN *WAS.*

WELL...THAT MADE *TWO* OF US.
IT TOOK A WHILE GOING FLOOR BY FLOOR, ROOM BY ROOM...

FLUSH!

...BUT I EVENTUALLY FOUND HIM.

NOW THAT I WAS THERE, I REALIZED THAT TAKING OFF THE CLOAK AND APPEARING IN THE MIDDLE OF HIS ROOM WOULD SCARE AMADEUS HALF TO DEATH.

I WAS TRYING TO DECIDE HOW TO HANDLE IT WHEN HE DECIDED FOR ME.
WELL? HOW LONG ARE YOU GOING TO STAND THERE?

I'M TALKING TO YOU!

HOW???

4D GOGGLES. THEY LET YOU SEE INVISIBLE, SPECTRAL, AND OTHER-DIMENSIONAL THINGS. YOU'RE NOT THE ONLY ONE WHO'S BEEN TO THE CELESTIAL SUPPLY SHOP.
YOU KNOW ABOUT THAT?
YEAH, MY DAD TAKES ME THERE. CLOAK OF INVISIBILITY, HUH? NICE. IS THAT A BOTTOMLESS BACKPACK?

ZIP!

...DELUXE.
FLIGHT ON DEMAND! KEWL!

IS ANYTHING SECRET ANYMORE?
BOUNCE!

SECRET ENOUGH. I MEAN, YOU'RE THE ONLY OTHER PERSON I'VE MET WHO'S BEEN THERE.
I WAS, WHEN YOU FIRST GAVE IT AWAY.
THEN WHY AREN'T YOU SURPRISED?

REMEMBER IN THE OLD FLEA MARKET, I SAID IT WAS THE SECOND TIME YOU'D SURPRISED ME? WELL, THE FIRST WAS WHEN WE WERE AT LUNCH. THERE'S ONLY ONE PLACE WHERE I'VE EVER HEARD ANYBODY SAY "GREAT GULA'S GHOSTS!" BEFORE.

THAT'S WHEN I KNEW YOU'D BEEN THERE.
MY BRAIN IS MELTING.

ANYWAY, WHAT ARE YOU DOING HERE? IF MY DAD FINDS OUT-

WHY HAVEN'T YOU BEEN IN SCHOOL?

MY DAD JUST WANTS TO WAIT UNTIL THINGS COOL DOWN A LITTLE. YOU KNOW. ABOUT THE WORM.

THAT'S WHY I'M HERE. AMADEUS, DID YOU HAVE ANYTHING TO DO WITH THAT?

IT'S HARD TO EXPLAIN. I DON'T WANT TO LIE TO YOU...

THEN DON'T.

IT'S NOT LIKE I WANTED TO. I MEAN...IT'S NOT ON PURPOSE-

WHAT ARE YOU SAYING?

THIS IS ALREADY COMING OUT WRONG. I DON'T KNOW HOW IT HAPPENED. THAT'S THE TRUTH! I SWEAR!
AMADEUS!

ARE YOU TALKING TO SOMEONE UP THERE?

NO, DAD! WHO WOULD I BE TALKING TO? I'M JUST...UM... PLAYING...

THERE'S SOMETHING STRANGE GOING ON... THE BARRIER WALL... THEN THE DOORBELL. I'M ACTIVATING THE SECURITY SYSTEM...

OH NO! YOU'VE GOT TO GET OUT OF HERE!
RELAX, I'LL SNEAK OUT THE SAME WAY I GOT IN—
NO YOU WON'T, NOT ONCE THE SECURITY SYSTEM'S FULLY ACTIVATED!

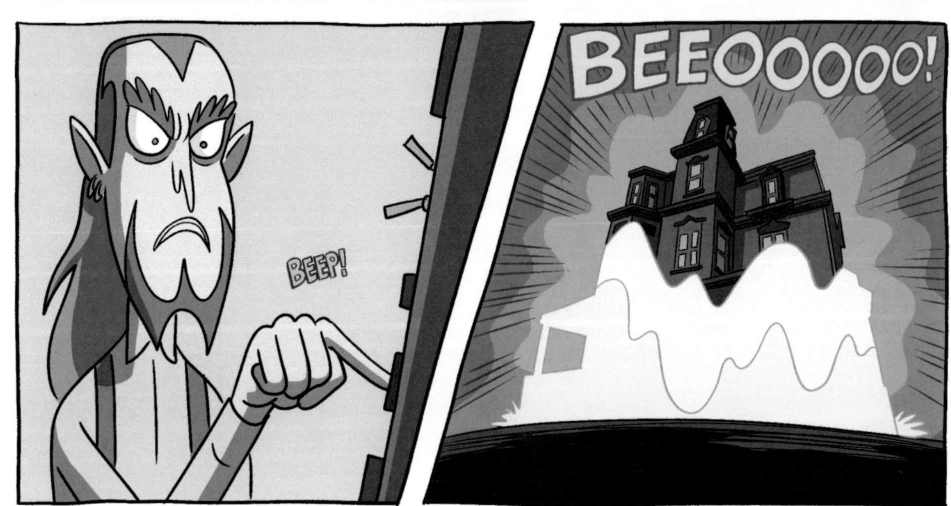
BEEP!
BEEOOOOO!

OKAY, WELL, HE'S GOING TO TURN IT OFF *EVENTUALLY,* RIGHT? I'LL JUST *HIDE* UNTIL-
TOO LATE!

NO, THAT'S TOO *DANGEROUS!* COME WITH ME, I KNOW A WAY. WE HAVE TO BE *VERY QUIET!*

IVOR!

TH-*THANK YOU,* IVOR!

KRANK!

GREAT GULA'S-
SHHHH!

DID YOU THINK YOUR HOUSE WAS THE ONLY ONE WITH A SECRET DOOR?
AS A MATTER OF FACT, UNTIL THAT MOMENT, THAT'S EXACTLY WHAT I THOUGHT.

THE PASSAGE LED DOWNWARDS FOR WHAT SEEMED LIKE *FOREVER,* DEFINITELY FARTHER THAN THE TWO FLIGHTS I'D COME UP.
WE WERE WAY UNDERNEATH THE HOUSE WHEN IT FINALLY *LEVELED OFF* AND WENT STRAIGHT FOR A GOOD, LONG STRETCH, UNTIL...

WOW! MY HOUSE DEFINITELY DOESN'T HAVE AN ESCAPE EXIT!
WOULD YOU KNOW IF IT DID?
HM. MAYBE NOT-
HEY! WHAT HAPPENED TO THE BACK OF YOUR HOUSE?

NEVER MIND THAT NOW. IT...HAPPENED A LONG TIME AGO AND MY DAD JUST NEVER FIXED IT. SEE WHERE YOU ARE? THAT WAY SENDS YOU BACK TO TOWN.
I KNOW, I'M FROM HERE.

LOOK, YOU DIDN'T ANSWER MY QUESTION.

I JUST... I DON'T HAVE ANY ANSWERS.

MY PARENTS THINK YOU HAD SOMETHING TO DO WITH IT. WHAT AM I SUPPOSED TO THINK?

...THINK WHAT YOU WANT, I GUESS. ALL I KNOW IS...I LIKED BEING YOUR FRIEND.

WHAT? WE'RE STILL FRIENDS, AREN'T WE?

...I DON'T THINK SO. DON'T COME HERE AGAIN, E.

IT'S NOT SAFE.
WAIT!

RUSTLE
RUSTLE!

RUSTLE!
RUSTLE
RUSTLE!

GUESS I PICKED A GREAT NIGHT TO LEAVE ROGER AT HOME IN BED!

RUSTLE
RUSTLE!
WHO'S THERE?
IF YOU'RE TRYING TO BE QUIET, YOU *STINK* AT IT.
RUSTLE!
RUSTLE
RUSTLE!
RUSTLE!
I'M NOT *AFRAID* OF YOU!
RUSTLE
RUSTLE!

SHOW YOUR-SELF!

WAAA! GROSS!
SKREE!
SKREE! SKREE!
SKREE!
SCURRY!
SKREE!
SCURRY!

BEOWULF'S BEARD!
SCURRY! SCURRY!
SCURRY!
A RAT KING!

EOWULF?

SNORE!
SNOOORRE!
SNORE!

SNORE!
SNORE!

SNOOOORRE!

I KNOW YOU'RE ASLEEP, BUT IT'S HARD TO REMEMBER THE LAST TIME WE WERE BOTH ABLE TO SIT STILL LIKE THIS. SEEMS LIKE YOU'RE ALWAYS RUSHING OFF SOMEWHERE.

I WANT YOU TO KNOW...
SNORE!
SNORE!

...I UNDERSTAND WHAT YOU'RE TRYING TO DO. I DON'T THINK THAT BOY HAS HAD ANYONE CARE ABOUT HIM, EVER.

YOU SEE SOMETHING THAT'S WRONG AND YOU'RE TRYING TO FIX IT.
SNORE!

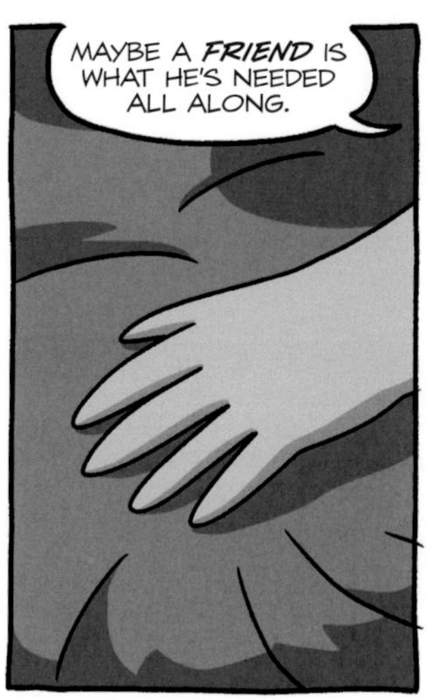
MAYBE A FRIEND IS WHAT HE'S NEEDED ALL ALONG.

THAT SUPERGROUP YOUR DAD BELONGED TO? THAT'S WHAT DROVE THEM APART, YOU KNOW? IT WASN'T ALL THE BAD GUYS THEY FOUGHT.
SNO--
--ORE!

THEY JUST WEREN'T ABLE TO SEE THE WORLD AS ANYTHING BUT A BATTLEFIELD, AND YOU CAN'T STAY AT WAR WITH THE WORLD FOREVER. YOUR DAD LEARNED THAT EVENTUALLY, BUT NOT FROM THEM.

THE GREATEST, HARDEST, MOST CHALLENGING ADVENTURES START WHEN YOU PUT THE WEAPONS DOWN. I DON'T REALLY UNDERSTAND WHAT HAPPENED ON THOSE ADVENTURES OF YOURS...

...BUT IT SEEMS LIKE YOU LEARNED THAT ON YOUR OWN SOMEHOW, AND YOUR DAD LEARNED IT FROM YOU, WHICH IS PRETTY AMAZING WHEN YOU THINK ABOUT IT–

NOW, IF I CAN JUST SAY ALL THAT SOMETIME WHEN YOU'RE ACTUALLY AWAKE...
SNORE!

WHAT...?
SPONGE! SPONGE!

ROGER!
WHERE IS SHE?
SNORT!

YOU KNOW I'D NEVER BETRAY HER.

"BETRAY"? I'M HER MOTHER, YOU GLORIFIED LETTER OPENER! YOU WILL FIND YOURSELF RUSTING AWAY IN THE DARKEST, DAMPEST CORNER OF THE GARAGE WITH THE OLD LAWN TOOLS NO ONE EVER USES!

YOU... WOULDN'T DARE!

TRY ME!

WAM!
MASH!
RROAARRR!

LEAVE HER ALONE!

AMADEUS, GET OUT OF HERE! THIS THING'S DANGEROUS!
NO! I CAN STOP IT!

UUUUGH...

ARE YOU OKAY?

RRAAAA!

WAAA!

SMASH!

THUD!

WHAT JUST HAPPENED?

GRAAA!

RUN!

SLLAMM!!!

GET UP! MOVE!

STOMP!

ZIM!

WHAT EXACTLY DID YOU THINK YOU WERE DOING BACK THERE?
YOU'VE NEVER WON A FIGHT IN YOUR LIFE!
I WASN'T TRYING TO FIGHT! I WAS TRYING TO SEND IT AWAY!
AND WHAT MADE YOU THINK YOU COULD DO THAT?

SLAM!
I JUST FELT I COULD!

SERIOUSLY? YOU COULD HAVE GOTTEN US BOTH KILLED! OF ALL THE TIMES TO SUDDENLY GET BRAVE, YOU SURE CAN PICK 'EM!

I'LL TAKE THAT AS A COMPLIMENT! NO ONE'S EVER CALLED ME BRAVE BEFORE!

BRAVE BUT STUPID!
WHAK!

RAAAAAAA!

HHHHHOOOOOOONNK!!!

SSSCCREEEE!

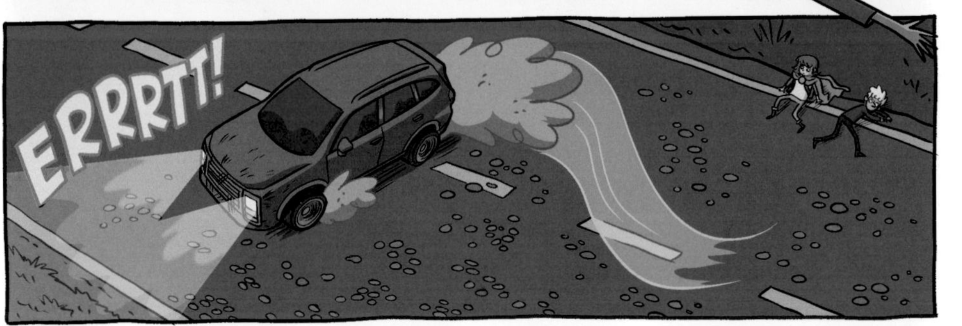
ERRRTT!

GET IN!

MOM?!

SCREE!
SCREE! SCREE!

IT'S RE-FORMING! HURRY–MY SWORD!

GET IN THE CAR NOW!

ARE YOU OKAY?
I THOUGHT I COULD TRUST YOU...
DID THAT SWORD JUST SPEAK?
HE JUST SAVED BOTH OF YOU, E! YOU OUGHT TO THANK HIM!
WHAT WAS THAT THING BACK THERE?

A RAT KING, I THINK...

AND WHERE DID THAT COME FROM?

NO IDEA, BUT IT LOOKS LIKE WE CAN SCRATCH AMADEUS OFF THE LIST OF SUSPECTS.
NOTED.

AM I GROUNDED AGAIN?

WHAT DIFFERENCE DOES IT MAKE? YOU DO WHAT YOU WANT ANYWAY...
IT'S NOT WHAT I WANT, I'M TRYING TO–
I KNOW WHAT YOU'RE TRYING TO DO!

AMADEUS, I OWE YOU AN APOLOGY.
THAT'S OKAY, MRS. WEGMUND...
NO, IT ISN'T. BUT WE'RE GOING TO TRY TO MAKE THIS OKAY SOMEHOW. WOULD YOU MIND IF I DRIVE STRAIGHT TO OUR HOUSE? I'D RATHER NOT HAVE TO TURN AROUND RIGHT NOW.
UM, THAT'S FINE.

YOU CAN CALL YOUR DAD WHEN WE GET THERE AND TELL HIM WHERE YOU ARE.

OH...YEAH, THAT'S OKAY. I MEAN, HE PROBABLY WON'T NOTICE I'M GONE...

SOUTH
9

3
IT'S ALL
RELATIVE.

WHOA.

UM... HELGA? WHAT...?
IT'S TIME, DEE. WE JUST NEED TO START SOMEWHERE AND EXPLAIN EVERYTHING.

BUT YOU SAID–
I KNOW.
WHAT ABOUT "NORMAL FRIENDS DOING NORMAL THINGS"?

THAT DIDN'T WORK.

WELL, I WISH YOU'D GIVEN ME SOME WARNING!
TEN MINUTES AGO, THIS PLACE WAS FULL OF SENTRIES...

THEY WENT TO CHECK OUT A SENSOR ALERT ON ROUTE 9, OR YOU WOULD HAVE WALKED IN ON THE WHOLE GROUP!

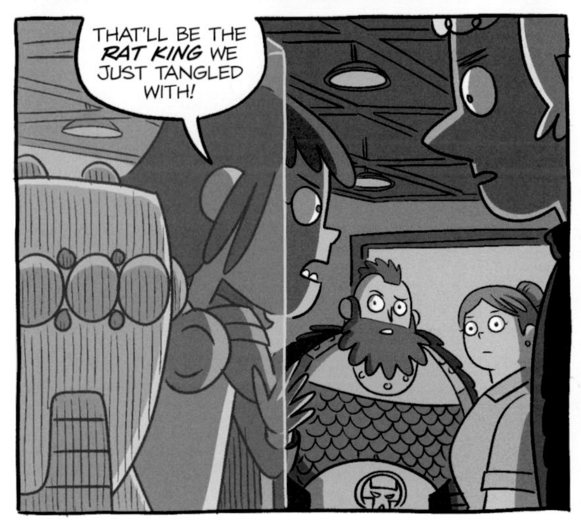
THAT'LL BE THE RAT KING WE JUST TANGLED WITH!

THE WHAT NOW?

YEAH, OUT BY AMADEUS' HOUSE.
WHAT WERE YOU DOING OUT THERE?
YOU'RE GOING TO HAVE TO ROLL WITH SOME OF THIS, DAD, OR WE'LL BE HERE FOREVER.
ANYWAY, IT WASN'T AMADEUS, AND I DON'T THINK HIS DAD'S GOT ANYTHING TO DO WITH THIS, EITHER.

WHY DO YOU KEEP SAYING THAT? STOP COVERING FOR ME!

I'M NOT. YOU DIDN'T HAVE A CHANCE TO MAKE THAT THING APPEAR. I WAS RIGHT NEXT TO YOU THE WHOLE TIME.
AND THEN, YOU HAD NO CONTROL OVER IT. WHOEVER'S DOING THIS, IT'S NOT YOU.

HOLD ON, YOU MAY BOTH HAVE A POINT. THIS DEFINITELY SOUNDS LIKE THE MISSING PAN PIPE!

THAT'S WHY I SAID TO START SOMEWHERE AND TELL THEM EVERYTHING!

ARE YOU SURE?

YEAH, I'M SURE. TRUST WORKS BOTH WAYS.

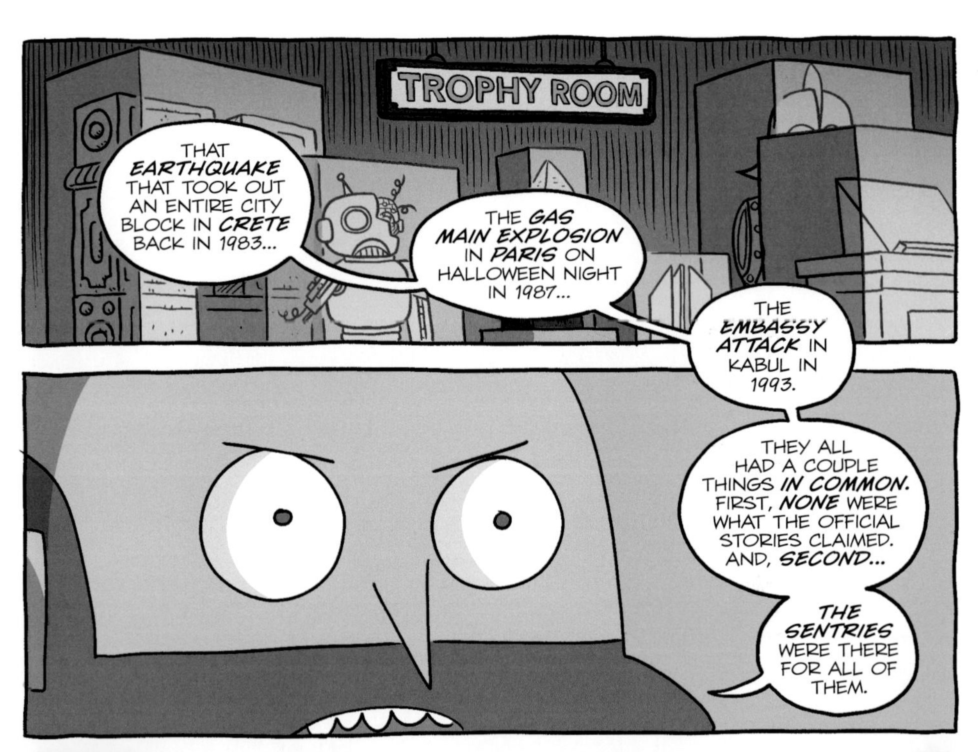
TROPHY ROOM
THAT EARTHQUAKE THAT TOOK OUT AN ENTIRE CITY BLOCK IN CRETE BACK IN 1983...
THE GAS MAIN EXPLOSION IN PARIS ON HALLOWEEN NIGHT IN 1987...
THE EMBASSY ATTACK IN KABUL IN 1993.
THEY ALL HAD A COUPLE THINGS IN COMMON. FIRST, NONE WERE WHAT THE OFFICIAL STORIES CLAIMED. AND, SECOND...
THE SENTRIES WERE THERE FOR ALL OF THEM.

ZENO LAMBROS TRACES HIS ANCESTRY BACK TO THE GENIUS INVENTOR DAEDALUS. AS THE ARMORED HERO ICARUS, HE PUT HIS KNACK FOR INNOVATION TO USE THROUGH AN AWESOME ARRAY OF ADVANCED GADGETRY.
HE'S ALSO YOUR FRIEND PHOEBE'S DAD, AND ONE OF THE WEALTHIEST MEN AROUND.

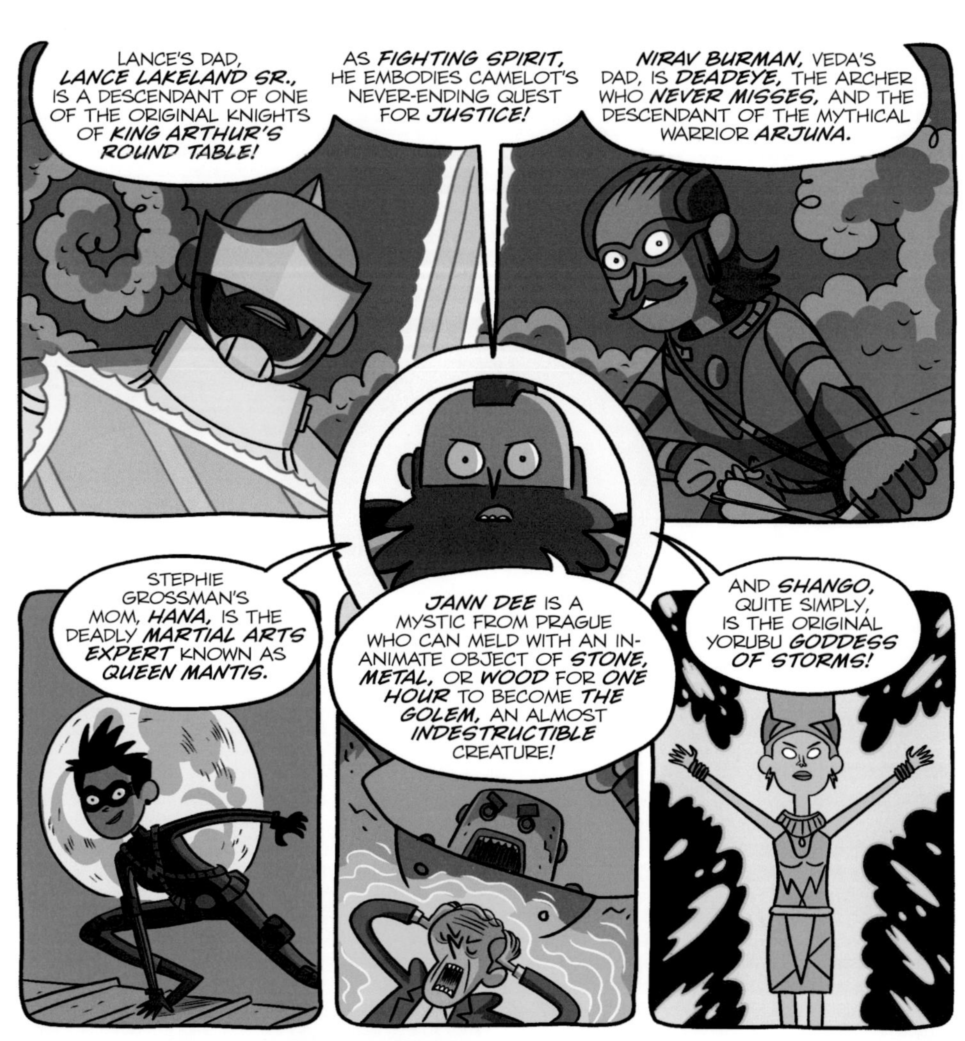

LANCE'S DAD, LANCE LAKELAND SR., IS A DESCENDANT OF ONE OF THE ORIGINAL KNIGHTS OF KING ARTHUR'S ROUND TABLE!
AS FIGHTING SPIRIT, HE EMBODIES CAMELOT'S NEVER-ENDING QUEST FOR JUSTICE!
NIRAV BURMAN, VEDA'S DAD, IS DEADEYE, THE ARCHER WHO NEVER MISSES, AND THE DESCENDANT OF THE MYTHICAL WARRIOR ARJUNA.
STEPHIE GROSSMAN'S MOM, HANA, IS THE DEADLY MARTIAL ARTS EXPERT KNOWN AS QUEEN MANTIS.
JANN DEE IS A MYSTIC FROM PRAGUE WHO CAN MELD WITH AN INANIMATE OBJECT OF STONE, METAL, OR WOOD FOR ONE HOUR TO BECOME THE GOLEM, AN ALMOST INDESTRUCTIBLE CREATURE!
AND SHANGO, QUITE SIMPLY, IS THE ORIGINAL YORUBU GODDESS OF STORMS!

THEN...PHOEBE, LANCE, VEDA, AND STEPHIE ARE JUST LIKE ME—THE DESCENDANTS OF LEGENDARY HEROES!
ISN'T THAT A LITTLE TOO COINCIDENTAL?

I'M GETTING TO THAT. GIVE ME A CHANCE.

SORRY, CONTINUE.

OUR MISSIONS WERE ALL EFFORTS TO STOP ONE BAD GUY OR ANOTHER'S EVIL PLANS, BUT THE WORST OF THOSE WERE AGAINST ONE WHO CALLED HIMSELF THE PIPER!

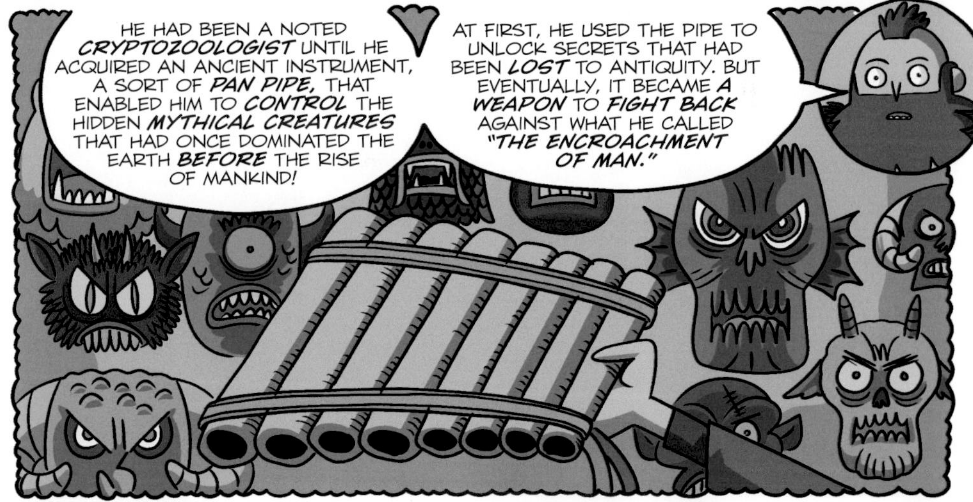

HE HAD BEEN A NOTED CRYPTOZOOLOGIST UNTIL HE ACQUIRED AN ANCIENT INSTRUMENT, A SORT OF PAN PIPE, THAT ENABLED HIM TO CONTROL THE HIDDEN MYTHICAL CREATURES THAT HAD ONCE DOMINATED THE EARTH BEFORE THE RISE OF MANKIND!
AT FIRST, HE USED THE PIPE TO UNLOCK SECRETS THAT HAD BEEN LOST TO ANTIQUITY. BUT EVENTUALLY, IT BECAME A WEAPON TO FIGHT BACK AGAINST WHAT HE CALLED "THE ENCROACHMENT OF MAN."

IF YOU HAVEN'T GUESSED IT ALREADY, THE PIPER'S TRUE IDENTITY IS... ASMODEUS HORNBURG.
WHAT?

I KNEW IT. BUT HE'S NOT THE PIPER ANYMORE!

WELL, SOMEONE IS! WE TOOK POSSESSION OF THE PIPE YEARS AGO–BUT IT'S GONE MISSING!

NOW IT'S ALL STARTING TO MAKE SENSE! YOU THINK AMADEUS SNUCK DOWN HERE AND TOOK IT THAT DAY WHEN HE WAS FOOLING AROUND IN THE MAP ROOM!

WHICH MEANS YOU PROBABLY ALSO THINK HIS DAD PUT HIM UP TO IT. AND THAT BECOMING FRIENDS WAS JUST PART OF THE PLAN TO GET IN HERE!

BUT HOW COULD THEY HAVE KNOWN ABOUT THE DOOR BEHIND THE BOOKCASE? EVER THINK OF THAT? OR ABOUT YOUR SECRET HEAD-QUARTERS? OR YOUR TRUE IDENTITY? ONLY ANOTHER SENTRY WOULD KNOW ABOUT ANY OF THAT!

EXACTLY RIGHT. BECAUSE BEFORE HE WAS OUR GREATEST ENEMY, ASMODEUS HORNBURG WAS ONE OF US– A SENTRY!

I DIDN'T KNOW THAT.

ON A MISSION IN SOUTH AMERICA, WE TEAMED UP WITH A MAGIC USER WHO WIELDED THE HELM OF HUITACA, AN ARTIFACT THAT GRANTED ITS WEARER THE POWERS OF THE GODDESS OF THE SAME NAME.
HER REAL NAME WAS SALOME SIMONE, AND AFTER THAT FIRST ADVENTURE, SHE JOINED THE TEAM ON A PERMANENT BASIS.
BOTH ZENO AND ASMODEUS FELL HEAD OVER HEELS FOR HER. AT FIRST, IT ALL SEEMED HARMLESS...
...BUT IT GREW INTO A DANGEROUS FEUD THAT THREATENED THE EFFECTIVENESS OF THE ENTIRE TEAM.
IN THE END, SALOME QUIT FOR THE SAKE OF THE TEAM, AND ASMODEUS WENT WITH HER.
IT WAS DURING THIS TIME THAT HE BECAME OUR ADVERSARY. HE REALLY SEEMED TO BE TRYING TO PROVOKE US.
THE FEW FIGHTS WE HAD WERE TERRIBLE, BUT THANKFULLY, HE SEEMED TO SNAP OUT OF IT...

...AFTER WORD ARRIVED THAT HE AND SALOME HAD WELCOMED A NEW ADDITION TO THE FAMILY.
THEN IT WAS ZENO'S TURN TO CRACK. HE WAS SURE THE CHILD WAS ACTUALLY HIS, AND HE SWORE HE'D NEVER LET IT GROW UP IN THAT HOME.

WHILE THE REST OF US WERE DEALING WITH AN ATTACK BY THE MAD ROBOTIC MONK, RASPUTNIK, ZENO TOOK HIS CHANCE.
AFTERWARDS, HE TOLD US SALOME HAD CALLED HIM FOR HELP. SHE WANTED TO LEAVE ASMODEUS, BUT HE WAS KEEPING HER PRISONER IN HER OWN HOME.

BY THE TIME WE GOT THERE, IT WAS ALL OVER.
THERE HAD BEEN A FIGHT, AND ACCORDING TO ZENO, ASMODEUS WOULD RATHER SEE SALOME DEAD THAN ESCAPING WITH A RIVAL.
WHATEVER HAPPENED, IT HAD BROKEN ASMODEUS. HE THREW THE PIPE AT US AND ORDERED US OFF HIS PROPERTY.

WE COULDN'T PROVE ANYTHING ONE WAY OR THE OTHER. SO...WE LEFT.

ZENO RAISED THE CHILD, YOUR FRIEND PHOEBE, ON HIS OWN. I HAVE NO IDEA HOW MUCH OF THIS, IF ANY, SHE KNOWS.

THE REST OF US SETTLED NEAR THE HORNBURG HOUSE, BASICALLY JUST TO WATCH AND WAIT.

WATCH AND WAIT FOR WHAT?

ZENO WAS CONVINCED ASMODEUS WOULD RETALIATE EVENTUALLY. BUT THE YEARS WENT BY, AND NOTHING HAPPENED. MOST OF US JUST GOT USED TO LIVING HERE, SO WE STAYED.

BUT SALOME SIMONE WAS MY MOTHER, NOT PHOEBE'S, AND I WASN'T RAISED BY ZENO LAMBROS!
BEE-DEEP!

ALERT! VISITOR AT FRONT ENTRANCE!
ANYONE EXPECTING GUESTS?
DING DONG!

THAT'S NO ONE I KNOW.

ME EITHER.
I THINK...

...I MIGHT RECOGNIZE THAT TRENCH COAT...

SAY WHEN.
WHEN. THANK YOU.

I'LL LEAVE THIS HERE. HELP YOURSELF.
YOU'LL EXCUSE US, ***MR. IVOR–***
UH, IT'S JUST ***IVOR.***
ALL RIGHT. IT'S JUST THAT YOUR ***STORY*** CHANGES ***EVERYTHING*** WE THOUGHT WE KNEW. I MEAN– ***TWINS,*** AFTER ALL!

THAT MAKES PHOEBE LAMBROS ***MY SISTER?!***
YEAH, THAT'S ***NUTS.***

EVERYTHING YOU ***THOUGHT*** YOU KNEW WAS BASED ON A ***LIE!*** I ***KNOW***–I WAS ***THERE!***

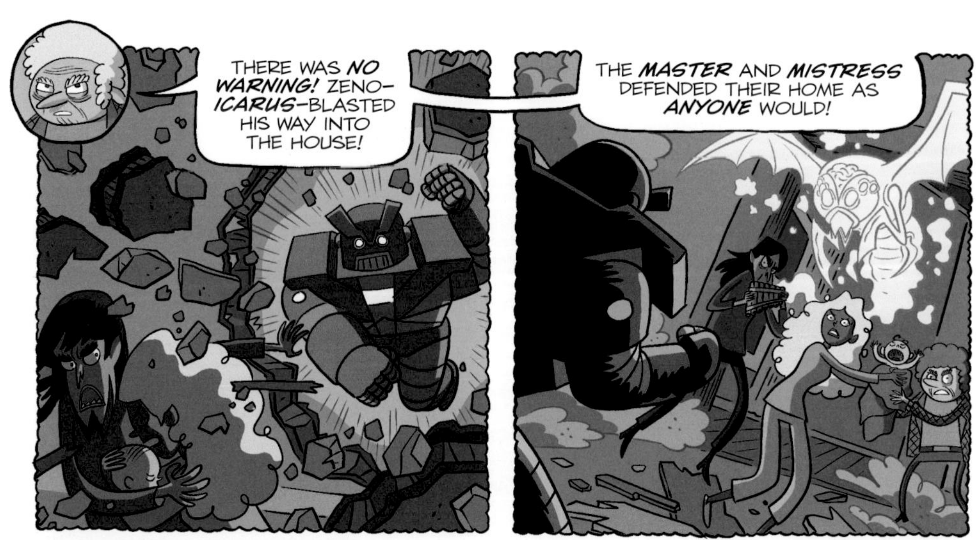
THERE WAS **NO WARNING!** ZENO-**ICARUS**-BLASTED HIS WAY INTO THE HOUSE!
THE **MASTER** AND **MISTRESS** DEFENDED THEIR HOME AS **ANYONE** WOULD!

THEIR **HOME,** AND **EACH OTHER!**

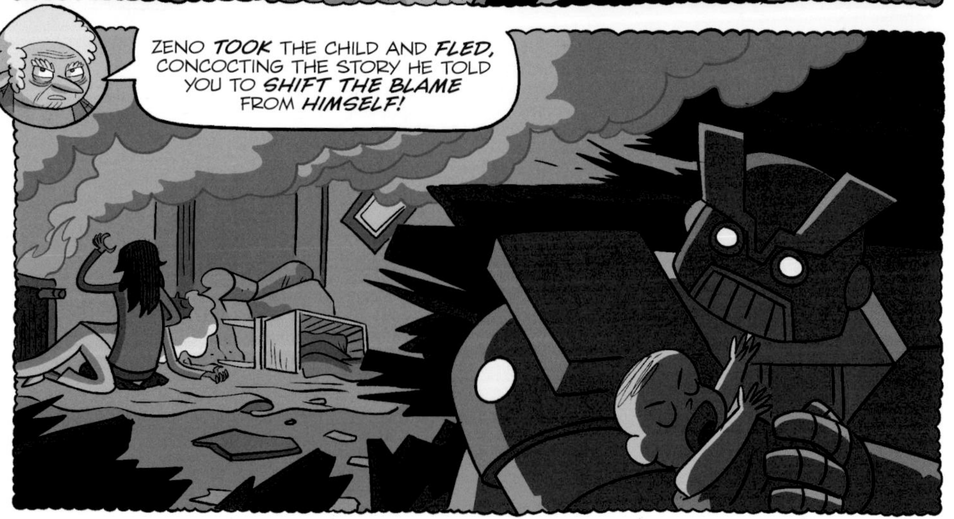
ZENO **TOOK** THE CHILD AND **FLED,** CONCOCTING THE STORY HE TOLD YOU TO **SHIFT THE BLAME** FROM **HIMSELF!**

BUT HE NEVER KNEW ABOUT MASTER AMADEUS—THE TWIN OF THE CHILD HE STOLE!
ASMODEUS NEVER FULLY RECOVERED. I DID MY BEST TO RAISE AMADEUS, THOUGH WE HOBGOBLINS HAVE DIFFERENT WAYS FROM YOU HUMANS...

YOU DID FINE, IVOR.

HM. RAISED BY A HOBGOBLIN. THAT EXPLAINS A LOT, ACTUALLY.

I'M JUST KIDDING!

SORTA...

WHY ARE YOU TELLING US THIS NOW, AFTER ALL THESE YEARS?
BECAUSE I CAN READ THE SIGNS!

THESE RECENT MONSTER APPEARANCES, THE SENTRIES ACTIVE AGAIN. JUST TONIGHT I SPOTTED THE REST OF YOUR TEAM ON THE BORDERS OF OUR ESTATE!

THEY'RE SEARCHING FOR THE RAT KING THAT ATTACKED EOWULF AND AMADEUS.
ASMODEUS HAS NOTHING TO FEAR FROM THEM...
ASSUMING HE HAS NOTHING TO DO WITH IT.

HE DOESN'T! SOMEHOW, YOUR FRIEND ZENO IS BEHIND ALL THIS!

ALL HE'S EVER WANTED IS AN EXCUSE TO FINISH OFF EVERYONE WHO KNOWS THE TRUTH ABOUT WHAT HAPPENED THAT NIGHT!

ZENO WOULD NEVER-

HAVEN'T YOU BEEN LISTENING? HE ALREADY HAS, ONCE BEFORE! WILL YOU LET HIM DO IT AGAIN...
AND STILL CALL YOURSELF A HERO?

I BELIEVE IVOR'S TELLING THE TRUTH.

DEE, SO DO I.

WHAT ARE WE SUPPOSED TO **DO?** GO UP AGAINST THE **WHOLE TEAM?** WE WON'T STAND A **CHANCE.**

WHAT IF WE COULD **CONVINCE** THEM THAT MR. LAMBROS IS BEHIND ALL THIS, **NOT** MR. HORNBURG? SHOW THEM **PROOF?**
WHAT **PROOF?**

THE PIPE! IF IVOR'S STORY IS **TRUE,** THEN MR. LAMBROS **MUST** HAVE IT.
IT WOULD HAVE BEEN **MUCH** EASIER FOR **HIM** TO WALK IN HERE AND TAKE IT THAN FOR **AMADEUS,** AND ALL THE **OTHER** PIECES FIT, TOO!

I SEE—WE'LL JUST HEAD OVER TO ZENO'S AND ASK IF HE STOLE THE PIPE, ATTACKED OUR HOME, AND TRIED TO KILL YOU AND AMADEUS...

...ALL WHILE COVERING UP THE FACT THAT HE CAUSED THE DEATH OF OUR TEAMMATE AND THEN STOLE HER DAUGHTER TO RAISE AS HIS OWN! THAT OUGHTA GO OVER WELL!

NO.
YOU GUYS HAD YOUR CHANCE TO SOLVE THIS A LONG TIME AGO. WHEN I SAID "WE," I MEANT ME AND AMADEUS.
OH, REALLY? WHAT ARE YOU TWO GOING TO DO?

RING THE DOORBELL.

WHAT ABOUT *THESE?*
OH. I FORGOT I *HAD* THOSE...

..."*THEWS OF THE HERO.*"
WHICH HERO?
WHO KNOWS? THAT'S JUST WHAT THEY'RE *CALLED.* THEY GIVE *ENHANCED STRENGTH,* THAT SORT OF THING...

I'M GONNA GO WITH *THOSE!*
OKAY, BUT LET'S WRAP THIS UP– YOU'RE TAKING *FOREVER.*

HOW DO I *LOOK?*
RIDICULOUS. LOSE THE *MAIL SHIRT.* THIS IS A *STEALTH* MISSION, NOT *A BATTLE.*

HOW COME *YOU* GET TO WEAR ARMOR?
BECAUSE IF WE *HAVE* TO FIGHT, *I'M* A FIGHTER. YOU'RE MORE OF A... *THINKER,* OR SOMETHING. BEST BET IS FOR YOU TO STAY LIGHT ON YOUR FEET.

FINE, **WHAT-EVER.**

HEY... I **KNOW** THAT LITTLE ROCK...

YEAH, I'VE ALWAYS WANTED TO **ASK** ABOUT THAT- WHY **DID** YOU STEAL THAT THING, JUST TO TURN AROUND AND GIVE IT **BACK?**

I GUESS...

...I JUST WANTED TO GET YOUR **ATTENTION.**

BEOWULF'S BEARD! WOULDN'T IT HAVE BEEN **EASIER** TO JUST SAY **"HELLO"?**

NO. **DEFINITELY NOT.** IT WAS **EASIER** TO STEAL THE ROCK.

YOU'RE A GENUINE WEIRDO, AMADEUS...

PROMISE YOU'LL NEVER CHANGE!

YOU GUYS ARE SURE YOU'RE UP FOR THIS?
WE'RE SURE.
IT'LL BE A CINCH!

DON'T GET OVERCONFIDENT. ZENO'S NO PUSHOVER.

DON'T WORRY, NEITHER ARE WE!

READY?
READY!
READY!

THEN HERE WE GO!

I HADN'T BEEN TO PHOEBE'S HOUSE IN A WHILE, BUT I STILL KNEW MY WAY AROUND PRETTY WELL.
I JUST ASSUMED MR. LAMBROS WOULD HAVE A SECURITY SYSTEM THAT WAS AT LEAST AS EFFECTIVE AS MR. HORNBURG'S.

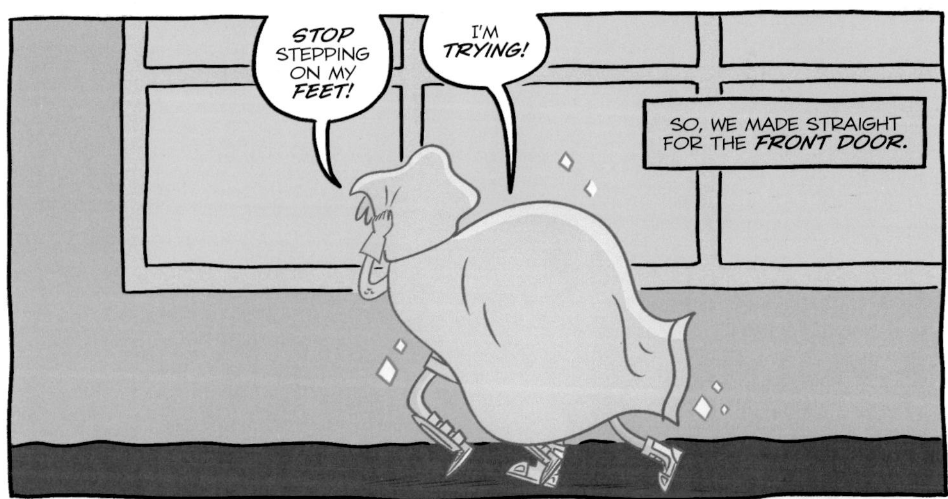
STOP STEPPING ON MY FEET!
I'M TRYING!
SO, WE MADE STRAIGHT FOR THE FRONT DOOR.

BONG!

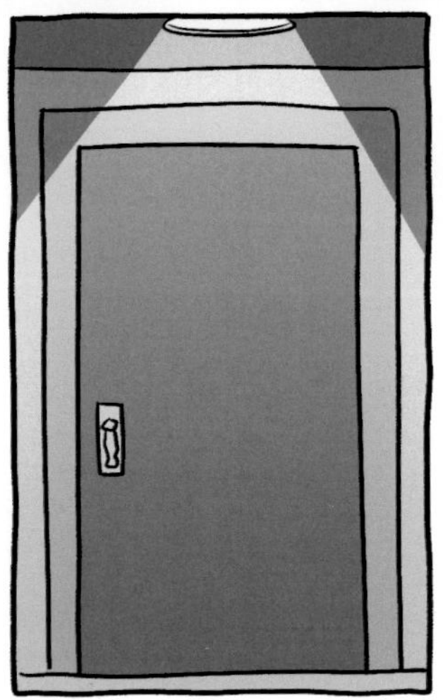

IT WORKED!
SHHHH! OF COURSE IT WORKED! NOW FIRE UP THOSE GOGGLES...

I'M GETTING... A LOT OF STATIC. YOUR CLOAK MIGHT BE MESSING WITH MY GOGGLES.
HMM. I DIDN'T THINK OF THAT...

MY OWN SCANS SHOW A HEAVILY SHIELDED AREA ON THE LOWER LEVELS. MY SENSORS CAN'T PENETRATE IT.
THEN THAT'S WHERE WE'RE GOING!

HOW ARE WE GOING TO FIND THE WAY DOWN, THOUGH, IF NONE OF OUR GADGETS WORK?
WE'LL HAVE TO CHANCE A PEEK. LOOK FOR SOME-THING OBVIOUSLY NOT OBVIOUS.

YOU MEAN LIKE THAT?

YOU'RE THE ONE WITH THE GOGGLES, YOU TELL ME...
THERE'S AN ELEVATOR BEHIND IT THAT ONLY GOES DOWN.
BINGO.

LOOKS LIKE IT'S THAT LITTLE STAR UNDER THE LEFT FOOT.

KRIK!

FWAAA!

ON THE WAY **DOWN,** I WONDERED ABOUT OUR DECISION TO GO **UNCLOAKED.**

WE HAD PASSED MR. LAMBROS **UPSTAIRS,** SO IT WAS SAFE TO ASSUME WE WOULDN'T BE BUMPING INTO **HIM** AGAIN.

THE **REAL** QUESTION WAS WHETHER ZENO HAD THE INSIDE OF HIS **OWN HOUSE** UNDER SURVEILLANCE.

PROBABLY, **YES.**

SO **THERE** IT WAS. I **KNEW** WHAT THE CAUTIOUS, **CAREFUL** THING TO DO WOULD HAVE BEEN. I JUST DIDN'T **DO** IT.

LOOKING BACK, I THINK PART OF ME **WANTED** TO GET CAUGHT. THERE WAS **A LOT** I WANTED TO SAY TO ZENO LAMBROS.

DING!
HERE WE GO.

WHOA!

WE'RE NOT HERE TO BE *IMPRESSED.*
WE'RE HERE TO FIND THAT *PIPE, CLEAR* YOUR NAME, AND *PREVENT ZENO* FROM TAKING THE SENTRIES *TO WAR* AGAINST *YOUR DAD.*
REMEMBER THAT.
SURE...

...WHO WOULD BE IMPRESSED BY *ANY* OF THIS?

WE TOOK IT ROOM BY ROOM...
...FLOOR BY FLOOR.
IT WAS IMPOSSIBLE TO KNOW IF THESE WERE **CURRENT** PROJECTS OR ALL **LONG ABANDONED.**
BUT ZENO HAD BEEN A BUSY GUY...
...AT **ONE TIME,** AT LEAST.
I WASN'T SURE HOW LONG WE WANDERED AROUND BEFORE THE HOUSE **FINALLY** BEGAN TO GIVE UP ITS **SECRETS.**

THERE'S **ANOTHER** HIDDEN DOOR BEHIND THIS WALL.

FFSHAK!

IT'S...
...SOME KIND OF HOLOGRAM.
...MY MOTHER.

UM...WE SHOULD KEEP MOVING...
HOW DARE YOU BRING HIM HERE?

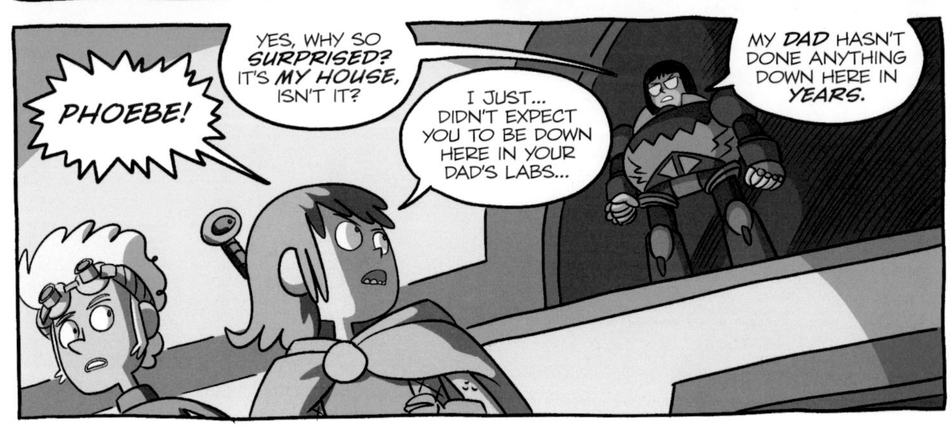
PHOEBE!
YES, WHY SO SURPRISED? IT'S MY HOUSE, ISN'T IT?
I JUST... DIDN'T EXPECT YOU TO BE DOWN HERE IN YOUR DAD'S LABS...
MY DAD HASN'T DONE ANYTHING DOWN HERE IN YEARS.

WHAT ARE YOU WEARING?

I'LL ASK THE QUESTIONS.

GOOD, BECAUSE I'VE GOT ALL THE ANSWERS, THOUGH I DOUBT YOU'LL LIKE THEM ALL THAT MUCH.

WHOA.
YOU...HAVE YOUR OWN ICARUS ARMOR!
LIKE IT? I MADE IT MYSELF.
BUT ICARUS IS MY DAD. I'M THE DUNGEON MASTER.
NOW...ARE YOU SURE YOU HAVE SOMETHING TO SAY I DON'T ALREADY KNOW?

AMADEUS AND HIS DAD DON'T HAVE THE PIPE. THEY DIDN'T SUMMON THOSE MONSTERS.

OF COURSE THEY DIDN'T.

I DID.

THE PIPE!
YOU?!
THAT'S RIGHT. I GUESS YOU DON'T HAVE ALL THE ANSWERS AFTER ALL.

IS SHE ALWAYS THIS SMUG?
PRETTY MUCH.

IT'S HARD NOT TO BE WHEN YOU'RE RUNNING RINGS AROUND EVERYONE ELSE.

RIGHT NOW, I'LL BET YOU'RE WONDERING ABOUT THE HEADACHES AND VISIONS YOU'VE BEEN HAVING, AMADEUS...

YOU KNOW, THE ONES THAT MADE YOU BELIEVE YOU WERE CONTROLLING THE MONSTERS? THAT'S JUST ANOTHER POWER OF THE PIPE–AND ANOTHER PART OF MY PLAN!

PHOEBE, CUT THIS OUT BEFORE IT'S TOO LATE. THIS IS NOT ONE OF OUR D&D GAMES– THIS IS SERIOUS!

THAT'S EXACTLY WHAT I INTEND TO REMIND EVERYONE!
"EVERYONE" WHO?

EVERYONE WHO WANTS TO JUST FORGET THAT MY MOM IS DEAD BECAUSE OF ASMODEUS HORNBURG!

THAT'S WHAT I'M TRYING TO TELL YOU, IT WASN'T MR. HORNBURG'S FAULT...

IT WAS YOUR DAD'S.

A STRAY BLAST FROM HIS ARMOR THAT WAS MEANT FOR MR. HORNBURG HIT YOUR MOM INSTEAD...
...AND HE'S BEEN COVERING IT UP EVER SINCE!

THAT'S A LIE.

YEAH? HE'S BEEN STANDING THERE LONG ENOUGH...
WHY DON'T YOU ASK HIM?

PHOEBE...
THAT ARMOR...
HOW...?
IS IT TRUE?

HOW CAN YOU ASK ME THAT? THIS BOY AND HIS FATHER HAVE CONFUSED YOUR FRIEND.

IT NEVER WOULD HAVE HAPPENED IF NOT FOR HORNBURG. WHO ARE YOU GOING TO BELIEVE? ME, OR THAT MONSTER LOVER?

WE DON'T HAVE TO BELIEVE EITHER OF YOU. THERE WAS ANOTHER WITNESS. ONE YOU DIDN'T KNOW ABOUT. AND HE SAW EVERYTHING.

WHAT WITNESS? YOU'RE BLUFFING...
I WISH I WAS. LOOK PHOEBE IN THE EYE AND SAY IT DIDN'T HAPPEN THE WAY I JUST SAID.
DAD, TELL THIS LIAR SHE'S WRONG.
IT...
IT WASN'T CLEAR WHAT HAPPENED...

WASN'T... CLEAR? BUT YOU SAID–

THE SMOKE, THE CONFUSION...

I HAD HIM! I HAD HIM RIGHT IN MY SIGHTS!

YOU WERE A HERO ONCE, MR. LAMBROS. YOU CAN STILL BE ONE.

TELL HER THE TRUTH.

SHE JUST...

...SHE JUST GOT IN THE *WAY.*

THERE'S *MORE,* PHEEBS...
WHEN HE *TOOK YOU* FROM THAT HOUSE...

HE MISSED THE *OTHER KID* THAT WAS THERE...

...YOUR BROTHER.

THAT'S— *THAT'S IMPOSSIBLE!*
IT'S REALLY *NOT.*

WHAT SHE'S *SAYING...*
IS IT TRUE?

DAD...?

PHOEBE...
YYAAAAAAAAA!!!
KRASH!

ZAM! ZAM! ZAM! ZAM!

PHOEBE, STOP!

VRRRRRRR!

I'M JUST GETTING STARTED!
ZWOOSH!

ARE YOU OKAY?
I'D BE **BETTER** IF I'D WORN THAT **MAIL SHIRT!**
HELP ME...

MR. LAMBROS!
I'M PINNED DOWN...

EOWULF, I'M **NOT** A **CROWBAR!**
IT WON'T BUDGE!

THOSE **THEWS OF THE HERO?** I THINK I REMEMBER **WHICH HERO** NOW...
OH? WHICH?

YOU!

KLANG!

STAMP!

STOMP

RRRIIIIIIIP!
WHOA!

RRAAA!

CAN YOU *WALK?*
YES, I'LL BE *FINE* NOW, BUT *PLEASE...*

...GO AFTER PHOEBE! SHE'LL NEED HER *FRIENDS* TONIGHT...

WE CAN FINALLY *AGREE* ON SOMETHING...
LET'S GO!

AMADEUS...

...I'M SORRY.

NOT HOW I THOUGHT TONIGHT WAS GOING TO GO DOWN, BUT THERE IT ALL WAS, OUT IN THE OPEN AT LAST.
MEANWHILE, OTHER THINGS HAD CLICKED INTO PLACE, TOO, SO I KNEW EXACTLY WHERE WE'D FIND PHOEBE.

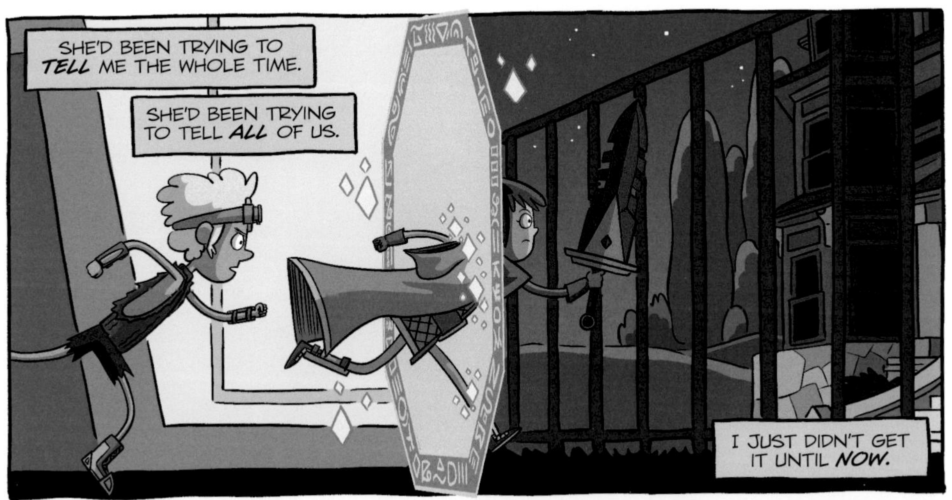
SHE'D BEEN TRYING TO TELL ME THE WHOLE TIME.
SHE'D BEEN TRYING TO TELL ALL OF US.
I JUST DIDN'T GET IT UNTIL NOW.

THERE WERE STEPHIE, LANCE, AND VEDA, FULLY DECKED OUT LIKE MINIATURE VERSIONS OF THEIR FOLKS.
PHOEBE WAS JUST WRAPPING UP HER STORY ABOUT HOW ANOTHER OF MR. HORNBURG'S MONSTERS HAD ATTACKED HER HOUSE AND INJURED HER DAD. AMADEUS WAS IN ON IT, AND I HAD SUPPOSEDLY GONE OVER TO THE DARK SIDE, TOO.

SHE HADN'T COUNTED ON US GETTING THERE SO FAST, BUT THERE WAS A SURPRISE IN STORE FOR ME, TOO.
I CAN'T BELIEVE THIS! YOU GUYS HAVE A TEAM? AND YOU KEPT IT SECRET FROM ME?!

NOW YOU KNOW HOW WE FELT EVERY TIME YOU FED US THAT UNUSED MOVIE PROP GARBAGE!
YEAH, WE KNOW ALL ABOUT YOUR "DESCENDANT OF BEOWULF" STUFF! AS LONG AS YOU HAD YOUR SECRETS, WE DECIDED TO HAVE OUR OWN!

I...DIDN'T THINK ANYONE WOULD BELIEVE ME...

AND NOW WE DON'T HAVE TO. YOU PICKED THE WRONG SIDE, E.
GUYS, I'M ON THE "LET'S NOT FIGHT" SIDE, OKAY?

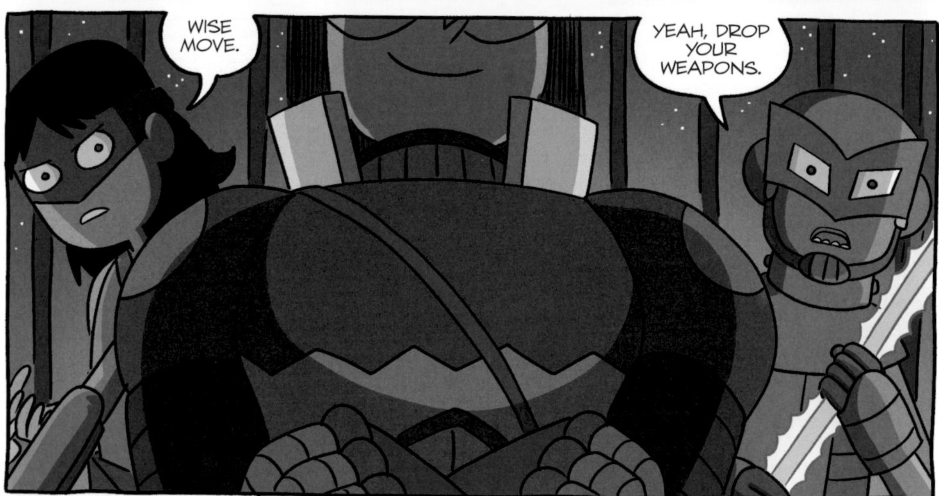
WISE MOVE.
YEAH, DROP YOUR WEAPONS.

PHOEBE IS LYING TO YOU. SHE'S BEEN BEHIND THESE MONSTER ATTACKS FROM THE BEGINNING.

SHE'S DONE ALL OF THIS TO GET BACK AT THE HORNBURGS FOR WHAT HAPPENED TO HER MOM, EVEN THOUGH HER DAD JUST CONFESSED THAT IT WAS HIS FAULT.

I GUESS YOU GUYS CAN BELIEVE ME, OR THE ONE WHO'S BEEN LYING TO ALL OF US ABOUT HERSELF FOR YEARS. I SAY TAKE THEM BOTH DOWN.

HOLD ON, WE'RE NOT YOUR PERSONAL HIT SQUAD. EOWULF DESERVES A CHANCE TO EXPLAIN HERSELF. WE OWE HER THAT, AT LEAST.

WE OWE HER NOTHING! THAT BOY AND HIS FATHER ARE CONTROLLING HER!

IF SHE'S BEING CONTROLLED, OUR JOB WOULD BE TO RESCUE HER, NOT FIGHT HER, WOULDN'T IT?

BEOWULF'S BEARD! I'M NOT BEING CONTROLLED, I DON'T NEED RESCUING, I'M TELLING THE TRUTH FOR ONCE, AND BY THE WAY, "THAT BOY" IS PHOEBE'S BROTHER!

RRRAAAH! DON'T SAY THAT!

STOP!

THIS HAS GONE FAR ENOUGH!
PHOEBE...

...SIT DOWN!

EOWULF IS TELLING YOU THE TRUTH. THIS WAS...

...ALL MY FAULT.

I HOPE YOU CAN ALL FIND SOME WAY TO FORGIVE ME...
NO...

NEVER!

PHOEBE, NO!

KRAK!

RRRRUUMMMMBBLE!

BLAAAARRGGG!

YOU KIDS STAY BY ME!
OKAY, BUT I THINK THIS CALLS FOR SOMETHING ELSE...

READY?
BORN READY!

<TRANSFORMATION SEQUENCE INITIATED>

WHOA!
ROGER, LET'S FIND PHOEBE AND SHUT THIS DOWN BEFORE SOMEONE GETS HURT!
ON IT!

ZAM!

FRA-KOW!

FINALLY! A WORTHY OPPONENT!
I BELIEVE I FOUND HER!

SECURITY SYSTEM'S ONLINE, SHIELDS ARE HOLDING.
NOTHING SHOULD GET IN HERE.

SIR, THOSE PEOPLE ARE OUT THERE FIGHTING FOR YOU...
AND AMADEUS.
SHOULD WE NOT HELP THEM?

I CAN'T HELP THEM, IVOR. THERE'S NO WEAPON IN THIS HOUSE THAT CAN STOP THIS.

WHAT THEY NEED IS A REASON TO PUT THEIR WEAPONS DOWN...

YOU HAD THAT, ONCE.

CAN'T YOU REMEMBER WHAT THAT WAS?

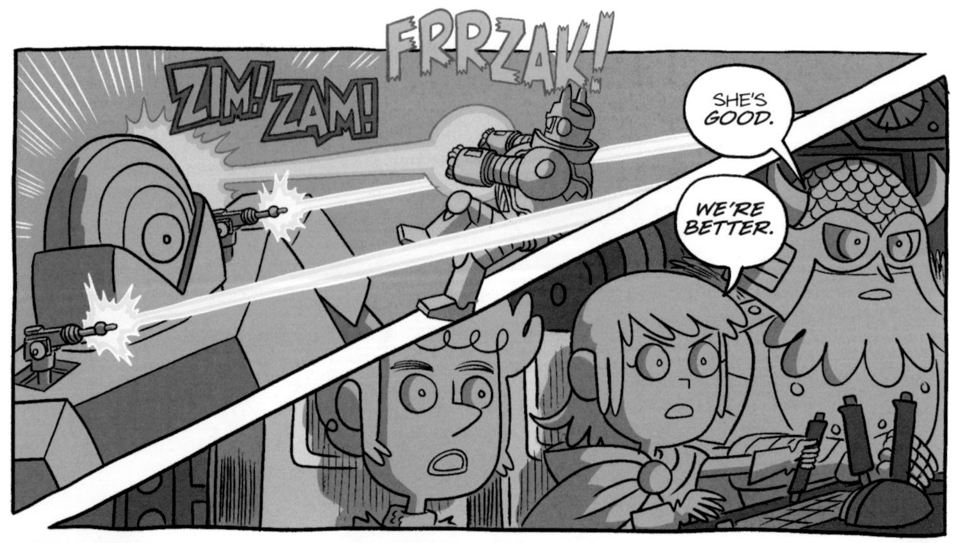
FRRZAK!
ZIM! ZAM!
SHE'S GOOD.
WE'RE BETTER.

PHOEBE, STOP THIS BEFORE SOMEONE GETS REALLY HURT!

THE SENTRIES COULD HAVE HAD JUSTICE FOR MY MOM YEARS AGO, BUT THEY LET THAT MONSTER OFF THE HOOK! NOW THEY'RE ALL GUILTY, AND EVERYONE'S GOING TO PAY!
ZRAKKA!

WELL, THEN I'M SORRY, BUT WE'RE GONNA FIGHT!
HM, YES, SOMETHING LIKE THAT...

WAM!
HA! HA! HA!

FFWAAASHHH!
KRASH!

HOW MUCH OF THIS CAN WE *TAKE?*
NOT A LOT. *DRAGON FIRE'S* PRETTY *INTENSE.*

RAAAAAAA!
ZAGGA!

SORRY I'M LATE...
THUD!

...I HAD TROUBLE GETTING THE CHARIOT STARTED.

MOM! I KNEW IT!
WAIT, WE HAVE A CHARIOT?

I KEEP SAYING YOU'VE GOT TO START IT UP EVERY NOW AND THEN OR THE BATTERY DIES...

OKAY, BUT WHEN WAS THE LAST TIME WE HAD DRAGONS?

WE'RE PINNED DOWN HERE... EVERYONE, STAND BY! I'M GOING TO DISENGAGE TO GET OUT FROM UNDER THIS THING. HOLD ON!

<TRANSFORMATION DISENGAGED>

AMADEUS, STAY CLOSE–WE'RE GOING RIGHT BACK TO GIANT ROBOT MODE!
NO, E...

...I WON'T SIT HERE AND LET EVERYONE ELSE FIGHT FOR ME– I HAVE TO FACE HER MYSELF!

NO!
GO AFTER HIM.

YEAH... THAT'LL TAKE A MINUTE...

KLANG!

WE CAN *FIGHT* IF YOU *WANT TO,* BUT–

AAAH!
GOOD, *THAT'S* WHAT I WANT!
ZABOOM!

THIS SHOULD BE MINE!

GIVE...
...GIVE IT BACK!

ALL YOU HAVE TO DO...
IS REACH UP AND TAKE IT!

RAAAAAAA!

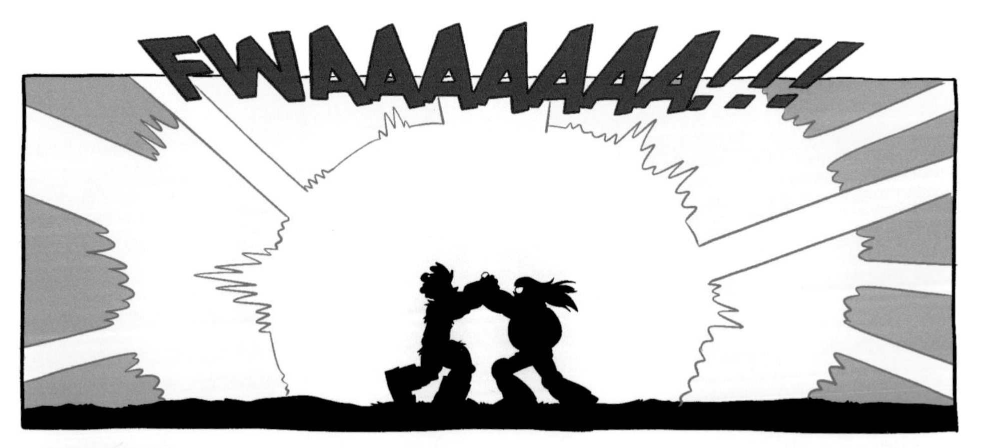
FWAAAAAAAA!!!

IT WAS ASMODEUS, BUT ALSO NOT ASMODEUS, BECAUSE HE WAS WEARING THE HELM OF HUITACA, THE ANCIENT ARTIFACT THAT HAD BEEN THE SOURCE OF SALOME'S POWER.
SHE WAS GONE, BUT THE HELM HELD A PIECE OF ALL WHO HAD WORN IT: THEIR LIVES, THEIR LOVES, THEIR HOPES, THE IRREPLACEABLE, INDESTRUCTIBLE MAGIC THAT WAS IN EACH OF THEM.

MEMORIES WOULD BE TOO SIMPLE A WORD. SALOME WAS REFLECTED—REVEALED—IN IT.
AND NOW, WHILE WEARING IT, SO WAS ASMODEUS.
THIS CURRENT SHOT THROUGH ALL OF THEM—MR. HORNBURG, AMADEUS, AND PHOEBE.
EACH ONE LIKE A PIECE OF A SINGLE BROKEN HEART. SALOME WAS NOT THE MISSING PART THEY ALL THOUGHT SHE WAS.
SHE WAS THE GLUE.
MR. HORNBURG HAD NEVER TRIED THIS BEFORE BECAUSE IT HAD SIMPLY NEVER OCCURRED TO HIM THAT SOMETHING OTHER THAN ANGER AND LOSS WAS NEEDED TO FILL THAT GREAT BIG GAPING HOLE LEFT BEHIND INSIDE ALL OF THEM.

SEEING AMADEUS AND PHOEBE **BATTLE IT OUT** ON HIS **FRONT LAWN** HAD DONE THE TRICK.
THAT, AND A LITTLE **PUSH** FROM **IVOR.**
THAT **PART** OF SALOME THAT WAS **PART OF THE HELM** FILLED, AND FILLED, AND FILLED, UNTIL THERE WAS **NO MORE ROOM** FOR **EMPTINESS.**

SHRAACKA!
SOMETIMES, WHEN A BROKEN BONE **HEALS WRONG,** THEY HAVE TO **BREAK IT** AGAIN TO SET IT RIGHT.

I THINK THAT'S WHAT HAPPENED HERE.

IT GLUED ALL THE PARTS BACK IN JUST THE **RIGHT WAY.**

DON'T GET ME WRONG—SOME OF THIS WAS GOING TO TAKE A WHILE TO SORT OUT.

THERE WAS SOME DAMAGE, SURE.

SOME THINGS WOULD NEVER BE THE SAME.

BUT...
...AN ADVENTURE THAT STARTED IN THE LUNCHROOM...
...WENT TO SEVERAL DARK PLACES...
...EXPOSED SECRETS, REVEALED MYSTERIES...
...MIXED UP MOST THINGS, AND SHATTERED THE REST...
...STILL MANAGED TO LEAVE BEHIND SOMETHING MORE PERFECT THAN ANYTHING THAT HAD BEEN THERE BEFORE.

IT HAD ALL
BEEN TRULY
EPIC.

Epilogue

CELESTINA ISLAND.
THE HOME OF VULCAN'S CELESTIAL SUPPLY SHOP.
...AND THAT'S ABOUT IT.
EOWULF ENDS THE LETTER SAYING "NOTHING WILL EVER BE THE SAME HERE—IT'LL BE BETTER!"

GREAT GULA'S GHOSTS, VULCAN! EOWULF'S RIGHT—THAT WAS AS EPIC AS EPIC CAN BE!
YOU'VE GOT THAT RIGHT, NICO. DEFINITELY NEXT-LEVEL STUFF!

HUMAN EMOTIONS REALLY ARE CONFUSING, AREN'T THEY, BOSS? IMAGINE WHERE THIS ALL MIGHT HAVE GONE IF EOWULF HADN'T FORCED IT ALL OUT INTO THE OPEN!

GOOD POINT, LULA. THAT STORY'S PACKED WITH HEROES, BUT THERE'S NO DOUBT EOWULF TOPS THAT LIST!

ALL THAT ASIDE, IT'S HARD NOT TO FEEL SORRY FOR HER, THOUGH.

HOW SO, BUCK?

IT WAS ALREADY A BORING TOWN TO BEGIN WITH...
THINK HOW MUCH WORSE IT'LL BE NOW THAT EOWULF'S SOLVED EVERYTHING!

HM. BUCK'S GOT A POINT. I WISH WE COULD DO SOMETHING ABOUT THAT.

WE SHOULD AT LEAST WRITE HER BACK AS SOON AS WE CAN.

DON'T WORRY ABOUT THAT, I ALREADY PHONED HER...
WHAT ABOUT, BOSS?

WELL, I WAS AS IMPRESSED BY ALL THIS AS THE REST OF YOU, AND I'VE BEEN THINKING WE COULD USE ANOTHER PAIR OF HANDS AROUND HERE, SO...

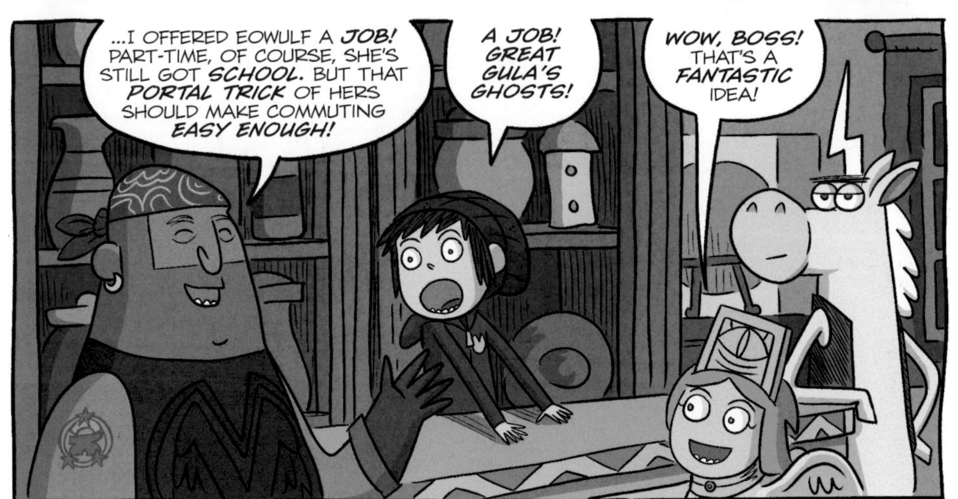
...I OFFERED EOWULF A JOB! PART-TIME, OF COURSE, SHE'S STILL GOT SCHOOL. BUT THAT PORTAL TRICK OF HERS SHOULD MAKE COMMUTING EASY ENOUGH!
A JOB! GREAT GULA'S GHOSTS!
WOW, BOSS! THAT'S A FANTASTIC IDEA!

WHAT DID SHE SAY?
WHEN DOES SHE START?
DID SHE SAY YES?
C'MON, BOSS– TELL US WHAT SHE SAID!
DOES THIS MEAN ONE OF US GETS PROMOTED?
OOO! PROMOTE ME!
WHAT DID SHE SAY?!?
THE END.
FOR NOW...